HEATH

Marshall's Shadow Book 5

KATHI S. BARTON

World Castle Publishing, LLC
Pensacola, Florida
Copyright © Kathi S. Barton 2021
Hardback ISBN: 9798498305950
Paperback ISBN: 9781956788099
eBook ISBN: 9781956788105
First Edition World Castle Publishing, LLC, October 18, 2021
http://www.worldcastlepublishing.com
Cover: Karen Fuller
Editor: Maxine Bringenberg

Prologue

James watched his target as they moved all around the restaurant. He wasn't there to end her life, such as it was, but to get her to a safe house, then go to his own home. There were all sorts of things she was going to be charged with, one of them treason to her own country. When someone sat across from him, he nearly snarled at his sister. Instead, afraid of her, he just ate his soup like he'd been expecting her all along.

I'm here to take over. He didn't bother looking up at her. The link they shared had it so that they'd have to never speak out loud if they didn't want to. *Someone has called your boss and said something has happened at your house, and you need to be transported home. Billy broke his leg in a fall from the bleachers at the football field at home.*

By the way she worded it, he knew that not

only was there nothing wrong with his son but that she'd already checked it out. When a bowl of the same soup he was sipping was set in front of her, she did what he'd done when he'd gotten his. Paige not only checked it for poisons but also smelled it to find out as well. When she pushed it away, he did as well, and unlocked the clip on his gun and put his hand on it at the ready.

Why were you called, do you know? She shrugged. Something she knew he hated, and she did anyway. *What's going down here? Anything I've done, or you?*

Both of us, as a matter of fact. She was eyeing the room, and he didn't bother looking too. Something he'd learned a very long time ago about his little sister, she was fucking good at her job. So was he, but he was too cautious, as he'd been told by her several times a day. *There are two geeks over by the door. They're trying their best to blend in, but they're not fooling anyone. Their language is too perfect, and they're dressed like peasants. Peasants can't afford bottled beer or the food they're eating. Not at the same time, anyway.*

Glancing in that direction, he took in as much as he could in the way of information. She was right, as usual — they were trying hard to blend. Also, he noticed that four other men were watching them and making no bones about how they didn't like them being there. He thought they were KGB but doubted he was right on that. The Soviet Union had nothing to do with this area, and the *Komitet Gosudarstvennoy Bezopasnosti* weren't the type to carry knives when guns were going to be needed.

"I think they're Feds. It would be just like them to come in and fuck up my day when I had such plans for the evening. Getting laid is far more fun without having someone firing over your head in a sleezy hotel room. Don't you think?" He just grunted at her. When she smiled, he wanted to laugh with her, but one of the Feds moved. "They're just going to walk right up to us and give all our hard work a day off too. Mother fuckers. Why is it that one hand, them, never knows what the other hand, us, is doing? Oh well. I'm going to bounce before they get here."

Sure enough, the man came and sat down in the chair his sister had only just vacated. Not removing his hand from the gun he had in his hand now, James looked around the room and then into the eyes of the man he was going to have to kill if he had fucked this up for him. Asking him in Russian what he wanted, the man didn't even know the local language.

"I asked you what the fuck you're wanting by coming in here. You should be sitting behind a desk and pushing shit around that you think you might be doing correctly. What do you want?"

"I have a message from my boss that I'm to tell

you." He didn't bother with asking the man who his boss was or even what the message might have been about. Wanting him gone, he looked slightly over the man's shoulder and into the eyes of his sister. The gun she put in the back of the Fed's head looked like she was trying her best to make it stay there forever.

"You're in my seat, moron." She spoke French to him. Even he could see he didn't have a clue on how to answer her. Then she tried any number of other languages she knew, which in his estimation was about all of them. "Who the fuck would send you into a war zone without you knowing a single language other than English? I am taking a fucking big chance here in thinking you might well know that one, but who the hell knows? What is it you want, jerk off? You have less than five minutes to tell me."

He didn't even get that long. Someone darkened the door to the shabby little shithole they were in and tried to kill everyone in there. James grabbed the woman he'd been there for when she'd been shot and let his sister fend for herself. He knew as well as Paige did that she had a better chance of getting out alive than anyone else. James was running down the row of houses behind the restaurant when he heard from her next.

"Is she dead? Should be, I'm thinking, for all the shit she's caused here." He leaned against the tree with the girl still on his shoulder and laid her on the ground. Checking her pulse, he told Paige she was alive. "Good. The Feds are all dead. Not only dead, but they were stupid enough to have worn their badges around their necks so anyone could see what a prize they got by killing them. I'm going to call their CO. Their commanding officer, or whoever the fuck is their boss, should have known better than to send idiots like this here. What did he want?"

"Don't know. Don't care. Where are you?" She told him. "How the fuck did you get up there? I'm assuming you know people that know people."

He laughed when she did, but he knew that to be true. Had it not been for Paige, he would have died a long time ago. As it was now, even getting injured was only a quick shift away from not being an issue again.

Paige had joined the service two weeks before he had. They had both gone through boot camp at the same time, but he hadn't seen her after the first couple of months there. James had thought she'd flunked out. But it had been her excelling in so much of the shit they had been teaching them that had gotten her looked at for more serious work than just a man with a gun.

I need for you to do something for me. He told her anything. *You still have a couple of contacts back home? I mean, someone you can trust more than you do me?*

I don't trust you at all, so that'll be easy. When she didn't laugh, he asked her what was going on. *I read the Fed's mind. You check in with your contact and let me know what they tell you.*

Should I be worried? She told him she was calling the CO of the other men. Not at all answering his question. *Really? Is that necessary, you think?*

I do. I'm hoping the Fed was wrong, and this was just another attempt to get you alone. He was beginning to worry now. When Paige told him to get back to her, he did something he'd never done in all his life — reached out for another person other than his sister.

Mr. Marshall? My name is James Avery. Can you give me some answers about what is going on there? The man broke down. James, unsure of what was going on, knew it had to do with his other sister and her little family, and he sat down. The car that was going to meet him here pulled up and took the woman away. *What's happened? Tell me, please?*

Your sister, Belinda Avery, she passed on a few days ago. James didn't know what to say but did ask if it had been Todd. *Yes. She was carrying his children when he beat her and those little girls of hers. My grandson – you might remember, he's a doctor – did all he could to save them babies. She had herself a little girl and a boy. Todd, he's in jail for attempted murder and murder. More to that, but I'm not privy to it right now.*

She's really dead? Mr. Marshall said he was powerful sorry about it but that she was gone. Had been buried just today. *I can't come home right now. I will, but I'm out of the country. I'll send my wife and family there to get things taken care of while I'm working on coming home. Thank you for getting her buried. Who's caring for the children?*

My family is right now. We didn't want them to be put in the system. Not that they might not end up there anyway, but for now, they're safe as hens' eggs in a nest. He loved the way Mr. Marshall had spoken. *You get yourself home here, and we'll hold off as much as we can. The house and its contents are being locked up. The murder, it happened at the house, you see. The little ones, the other two girls, they've been knocked around too, but they're going to be all right. I don't suppose you know where your sister is, do you?*

I'll find her. Mr. Marshall told him that would be good. *I'll be home in a week or less if I can get enough strings pulled. I haven't any idea if my sister will or not. She travels to a beat of her own drums.*

Yes, while I don't remember her much, I know all about someone doing their own thing. You let me know if I can help you with those there strings, James, and I'll see how hard they need to be pulled. All right? He told him he'd be fine. *You will be. I know it. I'll see you when you arrive. And let me know when you figure out your wife and family. We'll be putting them up, too, so you don't have to worry about that.*

After closing the connection, he sat there for a little while longer. Belinda was dead. Murdered by a man that all of them had hated. Now she had four children too, ones he'd never met in the first place. Looking up when a shadow fell over him, he saw Paige. Putting out her hand, he let her help him up from the ground. James started to tell her what he'd found out.

"Not here." Nodding, he followed her through the town for what seemed like miles. When they happened upon a house just outside the city limits, the two of them went in, and he was startled at not only how lovely the little home was but that it was air-conditioned. Looking at Paige, he asked her what was going on. "This is one of my hidey holes. Might as well be comfy when the bad guys are after your ass. Don't you think?"

"She's gone." When she nodded, he wondered who she had spoken to but didn't ask. Paige, like him, had contacts all over the world. Knowing about a sister in bumfuck Ohio, would be an easy thing to check out. "I'm going home. After I speak to Sara, I'm going to follow her there to find out what happened. Butch Todd killed her."

"He won't be anything anyone has to worry about soon enough." James didn't bother asking her. It would do him no good and only serve to piss her off. "I can't leave yet. I have two things going at once here, and I have to see them through. I don't know what I'd do there anyway but to kill Butch. He's going to die anyway, but that's all I can offer you at the moment."

"I understand." He did understand, better than most did, about his sister. "I was going to call Sara. Perhaps she can get us there and back without any issues."

When Paige left him standing there, he looked around the room. This was a room for a woman who didn't kill for a living. It was soft—the earth tones of the room suited his sister well. When she returned with a handful of money, he asked her where she'd gotten it.

"My stash. I don't get paid by check, as you know. I don't have a bank account other than the one that is in town for Belinda to use when she needed it. So I just stash it here. Other places too, but it's here when I need it." He looked at the stack. There were ten bundles of one hundred dollar bills. "It's a hundred grand. Just use it instead of your credit card. That way, no one will know where you've gone when you leave here."

"I could buy my own plane if this is all real." She didn't take the bait, nor did she give him any shit when he asked her how he was supposed to get around with this much cash. "What is it, Paige? I've given you ample lead way into busting my chops, but you've not bitten."

"The men that were sent to find you. They were sent by Harrison Parker." James sat down hard but didn't say anything. "She's in the FBI now. I called to speak to someone in charge of the two idiots that were here, and they told me that would be Agent Marshall. It didn't take me long to find out who she was."

"Marshall? You mean she's connected with the Marshall family of jags?" She only had to nod, and he felt blindsided once again. "How the hell did she get that gig? For that matter, how did we not know about this before? I thought we had enough tags on her to keep her in our sights forever?"

"I don't know, to be honest. I didn't talk to her, but I could have. I should have, actually." She looked at the doorway into a part of the house he couldn't see into. "I will, as a matter of fact. But here. Where I know she can't find me."

He didn't have to ask her what she meant. James knew Paige well enough to know that if she told you no one would find her, no one would. Ever. He knew too that even if a person were walking right over her, they'd never know she was right there beside them until it was too late. Looking at the money again, he wondered what was going to happen next. Because something was always about to go down while they were dealing with bad situations in their line of work.

By the time he was ready to go back onto the streets, he not only had a way back to the States, but he had two months off with pay. Whoever his sister had contacted on his behalf, they had fallen all over themselves getting him home. James asked her if she was going to be all right.

"I could have killed him six months ago. He was right there in my sights, and I could have blown his fucking head off, and no one would have been happier about it than me." He asked her what had happened. "Belinda. She asked me not to do it. Said that it would haunt her if I did. I told her he was going to kill her someday, and she told me that it was her lot in life. But that if he would die now, by the gunshot to the head, she'd lose her babies because no one would ever believe she'd not killed him."

That was true. Belinda had been trying her best to leave Butch for years. The man would drag her back every time, hurting her and the girls more each time. When Paige told him to go, to be careful, he knew she'd have to deal with this on her own. Paige would carry the guilt to her grave if she really thought it had been her fault their sister was dead because of something she'd not done when she could have.

~*~

Rodney ate his dinner in the kitchen, watching television with their cook. After he was finished, he went to the living room to take a nap. He loved the fact that there wasn't a television in this room. Rodney could do whatever he wanted, nap or read, and there were no distractions. Hell, he could—

"What is it?" Rebel appeared in the room with him, and she had a man over her shoulder. Taking him from her, she disappeared again, this time returning with a woman over her shoulder. Taking them up to the bedrooms, he put the man on the bed and began undressing him to see where all the blood had come from.

"Where am I?" He didn't get a chance to answer the man before he started telling him he couldn't tell anyone he was there. Not even his family. "The woman that came for us did she get my sister too?"

"Yes. I didn't see much of her, but she's in the other room." The man closed his eyes, only to open them a few seconds later. "Where are you hurt?"

"I'm shot, but I just need to shift. I'm all right. Go to my sister, she's not all right. Nor can she shift right now. It'll weaken her more." Nodding, he asked the man if he could do anything for him now. "No.

I'm just desperately wanting Paige fixed up. Go on, I'll be all right. I swear to you."

After checking the wound that had indeed been a through and through, Rodney went to the other room to help Rebel. The woman in there would not be able to shift her wounds away. Nor would she live long if she even tried to shift into whatever she was. It occurred to Rodney that he had no idea what the man was either. Helping Rebel, he told her what he'd found out about the man.

"Which is very little. How about you?" Rebel told him where she'd gone and how she'd found the two of them. "You just entered a warzone and got them both here? Christ, that's amazing. I'm proud of you."

"Don't be. I have a feeling that if either of these two dies, we're going to be on a long list of shit jobs for the rest of our days." Rodney asked her if she knew who the woman or man was. "Nope. I mean, other than a name, nothing. She's Paige, and he's James. All I heard about them as I boogied out of there with him. When I returned for her, I had to break her out of a jail cell that looked like something you'd see in zoos. Where you'd want to keep the animals that misbehaved a great deal."

They worked on Paige for nearly three hours. Setting up an IV was the hardest part. Nothing would penetrate her flesh very well. Finally, they had to resort to using a very large needle to make the mark, then stab it into her that way. The two of them put nearly four hundred stitches in her body alone. Her legs and arms were a different matter altogether.

As they were finishing up, James came into the room looking as fresh as a daisy. "I hope you don't get too upset with me. I put a couple of scratches in your flooring. I'll pay for its repair." Rodney told him not to worry about it. "How is she doing? I've never seen her down before. In all the years we've worked together, I've never seen her wounded or even hurt with a broken nail. This is scary for me."

"Are you related to the people at my brother-in-law's house?" He told Rebel he was their father. "They're good and well trained. I have to admit that to you. When I went there to talk to Harris about something, I was down on the floor and spread out before I even knew there was anyone else in the house."

"Good to hear. Just because they're on domestic soil doesn't mean they should be lax. I'll have to tell them what you said." She nodded. "Is she going to make it?"

"Yes. For the simple reason that she's an immortal. However, you weren't when I got there to get you." He said he didn't think it was in the cards for him to live forever. Then he looked at her sharply, asking her what she meant by her statement, "The vampire there when I arrived, the person that was with you two watching over you, they gave you enough blood that put you over the edge of immortality."

"Fucking bastard." James said he was sorry for cursing. Rebel told him it was a second language for her. The three of them laughed. "He said he'd watch over us until you came. I don't know how he contacted you, but I'm—"

"He didn't. Your sister did." He asked her what she meant. "She's part witch. I don't know how strong—all I can feel from her now is pain. But her being injured this badly called out to me. Had you not been there with her when I arrived, I would have left you for dead. But she told me you were to come here first. I did what she wanted."

"I don't understand." Rebel told James she didn't either. That she was a grand witch and that the two of them must be important to someone higher than her. "I don't know who it would be. I mean, there are any number of people watching out for us, but as for her calling to you, I don't know."

"We'll get answers when she's ready to give them. For now, we'll keep it quiet that you're here with her." James nodded. Then he sat down in the chair by the bed and held his sister's hand. "Your family, won't they miss you?"

"No. They know that when I want them to know where I am, I'll tell them. As for now, we have to assume that someone knows she's hurt and I am with her. The fewer people knowing that, the better." He looked at the two of them. "I'm sorry I can't give you more information. But it is literally a matter of national security that we aren't found or killed."

"I can live with that. I can use a little magic to keep anyone from coming into this room. There is staff that you might hear. Also, and this is a biggy, if I tell you to move your ass or anything else that will keep me and mine safe, you'd better fucking know that I'll hurt you badly if you don't. Deal?" He laughed and told Rebel he understood. "Good. Then we should get along just fine and dandy."

Rodney didn't know what was going on. But so long as everyone was working well together, he was fine with that. But all bets were off if anyone came here with the thought of hurting his family. That would include the kids at Harris's home. He had an entire shadow that he'd bring around if anything happened to anyone.

Chapter 1

There wasn't that much going on right now. Thankfully, Heath thought, his house was going to be done soon. He'd spoken to Harris, and she had not only hired a larger crew to finish up his home before winter settled in but also had him going through the barn looking for things to fill it out with. The other day he'd ordered linens, dishes, pots, and pans. Most of it would arrive tomorrow. Hopefully. Heath was sick to death of eating off paper plates.

"Can I help you?" He turned around to find a man without a shirt on and barefooted. His body wasn't scarred, but he did look fit and ready to take on a battle. Heath didn't know him but wasn't all that worried right now. The other man had been exercising, Heath guessed. "I don't know you, but you're also a jaguar, so I'm assuming you're related to the people that own this barn."

"I'm Heath Marshall. I was looking for some dressers I was told went with the beds I found here the other day. Who are you?" Instead of answering him, the man put out his hand. Heath looked at it, then at the man. "Nope. You talk, and I'll think about letting you into my head."

"James Avery." Heath nodded but still didn't take his hand. "Rebel and her husband Rodney have been hiding my sister and me away for the last two weeks. She's the grand witch, Rebel is, and her husband—your brother, I'm assuming—is her familiar. You have a grandda named Sheppard that is very talkative. He's been helping a woman by the name of Shannon Hutchison since she lost her mother about the time we were brought here to be hidden away. I know this information could have been gotten from anyone around here, but I'm trying not to cause trouble after all that's been done for myself and my family."

"Your sister, you said. Where is she?" He said she was recuperating but not up and around just yet. "I still don't trust you, Mr. Avery. But for now, I guess I have no choice."

"All right. I can live with that. The dressers are over at the other end of the barn. They're marked as to what set they go to. I don't know who put this stuff out here, but they certainly did a good job of ensuring it was safe and well cared for. Even in the barn." Heath turned to head that way but paused, then cocked his head and looked at the man. "Something else?"

"There is a younger male out here with you. I'd say about ten or so. He needs to use deodorant — the unscented sort, or he's going to be found every time he tries to hide. Also, he should never use lotion when he's out on the job. Wait, not lotion, but some sort of antiseptic. Harris would have kicked his ass had he been working for her." James whistled, and the boy came down from the rafters with a gun over his shoulder. He looked feverish and slightly pale — at least he did to Heath.

James asked the boy if he'd heard what Heath had said. "You could have gotten us both killed with mistakes like that. Be careful next time, all right?"

"Yes, sir." The kid didn't put out his hand when he was down the ladder but held onto it tightly. Nor did he make eye contact until Heath told him to look at him. Without thought to what James might think, he spoke to the other man.

"He's in pain. Not a great deal — I'd say a broken rib or two. Also, there is a cut on the back of his leg that is festering. Normally I'd not know to smell any of this, but Harris is rubbing off on me. Also, you more than likely smelled it as well, but since it probably has worked up to the level of infection now, you didn't notice it. You might want to check to see if he has allergies. I think the straw has given him something. There are no rats around here, as you well know, but this boy is hurting." James asked him if he could tell how he'd been hurt. "No. I'm sorry. I won't go into his mind unless it's necessary. It doesn't seem to be anything I need to look into since you seem to have a good relationship with him."

"Thank you." The boy, his name was Billy, as it turned out, was asked about his wounds. After telling his dad what had happened, that he'd fallen in the rafters a few days ago, the kid leaned over and puked up blood. "Christ."

Rodney met him in the barn when he was able to get the kid to the ground. Shaking now, he looked as if he was fighting a fever and had been for a few days. His body was clammy and sweaty at the same time. Just as Heath was pulling off his shoes to check on the wound on the back of his leg, Rodney handed him a pocketknife to cut through the material of his worn yet still in good shape jeans.

"Jesus." That was as good a word for it as he'd have said. "How long has he been walking around with that? It looks like it's gangrenous. Did he say anything to either of you?"

"No, he didn't. How did he get an infection in the—? Found it." Rodney flipped the boy over and touched the infected area. When a long sliver of something came out of the wound, so did a dark pus. "You look for more of it, Heath, and I'll give him something for pain. He's got to be hurting pretty badly right about now."

Billy was out in seconds. Digging around deeper into the wound, Heath was able to pull out three more pieces of what looked like straw and set them aside. Once the wound started to bleed, he knew it was getting cleaned out. But there was still the infection to worry about.

Rodney worked on the boy for an hour with his help. After they did what they could in the barn, James picked the boy up and carried him to the house as soon as he was given permission to do so. When he was laid out on the bed, the two of them stripped Billy down to his boxers and started wiping the wound on his leg down. The bruising on his ribs was massive, but Heath wasn't a physician, so he kept his mouth shut.

The woman that came into the room was obviously too weak to be up and around. The second time she fell against the furniture in the room trying to get to the bed, James ordered her to sit down. The look on her face made Heath think she wasn't thrilled about being yelled at, but she did sit in the chair.

"Christ, Paige. What the hell do you think

you're going to help with if you're barely able to stand on your own? Just sit there and try not to worry me more, all right? I have enough to worry about with Billy being so ill." She said she was sorry. "I know, honey. I'm sorry too. I shouldn't have snapped at you either. I wouldn't have known he was ill had it not been for this man. I'm still worried."

"I'm going to set him up with an IV to flush out his system. Now that the wound is cleaned of foreign objects — at least I'm hoping so — he should feel better in a few hours." James asked Rodney about his ribs. "I have to wait until my machine gets here to do some X-rays. I'd say he's had those since he got the wound on his leg."

Rebel came into the room and smiled at them. "He has been nursing his leg for the last ten days. Billy has fallen a couple of times against the furniture in his room when the pain takes him under. It never occurred to me that he was hurt, as he's been not bathing. However, I think it's what Rodney said — we've been around him since the beginning, and we never noticed anything different." James told Rebel that he'd been told that already. "I'd say he was more than likely doing that on purpose so no one would smell his infection. He'll be able to shift as soon as he's stronger."

"Like me." Heath turned to the woman in the

chair when she spoke. She, despite being beautiful, looked like shit as well. "I can read your mind. So if you want me to not make up a list of shit that I'm going to beat the hell— Well, fuck a duck and watch it waddle. You're my mate."

"Am I?" She nodded, and he stayed where he was while she cursed. Heath thought for sure that she'd cursed him in seven different languages but kept his mouth shut. When she stopped and stared at him, he smiled. "I'm not sure I can be as unhappy as you are about this, but I'm Heath Marshall. You must be Paige Avery. I've not heard anything about you, but James said you've been here for a couple of weeks."

"I was shot to fuck on the job." He said he could see that she was still weak with it. "Rebel said there is some witch in me as well, but unless Boddy pulled a fast one on me, I had no idea he left something else behind when he gave me a little of himself. Don't you fucking hate it when you can't even trust a fucking witch?"

He wasn't sure what to say to her, as he was related to the big witch. Both Rodney and Rebel were witches, Rebel, the grand witch. When Paige laughed, he did as well. Looking at Rebel when she said his name, she explained to him how no one was to know they were here yet. They were being hidden from someone higher on the food chain than even Harris. That was scary. He thought the only person higher on the food chain than Harris was the president. But he'd talk to her about it later.

There was more infection in Billy's wound. After slicing up his leg more, Rodney had Heath keep the wound open so he could dig around. He found a total of five more pieces of straw after what he'd pulled out earlier. The kid must have been shoving it up in there, was all he could think about.

"He didn't." Looking at Rebel when she sat down in the chair that Paige had been in, he noticed for the first time that Paige was gone. While he didn't know where she was, Heath hoped she was resting. "He'd been up in the loft looking around the landscape. Falling back when a bird dove into the opening, he slammed his leg up against one of the nails on the floor. The straw worked itself into his wound then as well. The sticky substance on the nail made it, so there was a lot of straw on it. When he pulled the nail free, the straw, dirty and dusty, stayed behind. He's very lucky you smelled it when you did, or he might well have lost his leg."

"Paige is my mate." Rebel nodded but didn't say anything more. "She told me. I hadn't been close enough to her to get the scent. What can you tell me about them being here?"

"I can't tell you anything, I'm afraid. I know a great deal — more than likely more than either of them do. But telling you would be dangerous. Not for them, but for you." Heath nodded but didn't ask. "Harris knows as well. She's upgrading your home for you as we speak. I guess something is going on that few people know about."

"But you." Rebel nodded at him. "Okay, so I have a mate that has something to do with national security. Someone on the food chain, I was told, is out to get her and her brother. Who, I might add, has three children that scare the shit out of me. Also, and this one is really strange, all of them, including this one, have been changed by Paige to keep them safe. Did I miss anything?"

Rebel stood up. "Yes, but as I said, nothing I can tell you. But, and this one thrills me to no end, there is no husband coming after her for anything. No family to speak of that is still living but a brother and his kids. He had a wife, but she was killed not long ago, I guess. So you don't have her coming after you either. You've no worries that there is someone related to them that is after her. She's a ghost, a shadow, and if she didn't want you to know she was standing right next to you, you'd never know she was there. So I have to think the two of you will be safe no matter what Harris does for you." He asked if she thought he'd need to be safe.

"All of us do, Heath. Also, you can bank on one thing with this family. We love with all that we have and will die protecting those we love."

He sat with Billy until his father returned. Heath thought about asking him about Paige but decided that wasn't the right thing to do. Standing up, he decided he needed to go back out to the barn to finish up. But on his way out, he slipped into the room Paige was in and was startled to see her lying on the floor. She was all right, she told him, just stretching her back.

"I'm sick of being idle if you want to know the truth." Heath helped her up from the floor and then to the chair. He told her he didn't care for it either. "Can you take me on a walk? Not far, I guess, or my brother will have a fit. But just out into the crisp weather so I can hear the leaves crunch under my shoes."

~*~

"You don't speak much, do you?" Paige looked at the handsome man standing next to her. They'd been outside for nearly two hours, and he'd not said much more than a handful of words. "I mean, it's great that you're not a chatterbox, but do you have anything to ask me about anything?"

"Plenty, to be honest. So many things I can't wrap my head around any one subject." He asked her if she wanted to have a seat. The bench there was just what she needed. "What division do you work for? I mean, will you be able to tell me that? How did you get shot to fuck, as you called it? I have a house. Would you like to see it? See, I have my mind going around in circles, and it's making me a little dizzy."

"Yes, I can tell you whatever you want to know. To a point. Until I figure out who shot me. Or who hired someone to shoot me. Divisions? All of the branches, I guess you can say. I'm not just a part of the Delta Force crew but also a Navy Seal. Special Forces mostly, but I get around." Heath asked her if she spoke a lot more languages than the six or seven he'd heard. "Yes. Translate them as well as read and write them. I have a special knack for that and languages, I guess you could say."

"Rebel brought you here and said you were immortal when she arrived to pick you up. Also that you have Wiccan in you." She nodded but didn't know how much she could tell him on that. "I'm all right with not knowing everything, Paige. I truly am. However, knowing enough to help you keep the two of us safe would make me feel a good deal better about this. I know you can pretty much kick the ass of anyone that comes after you. I can't. I'm just a nerd that works on computer programs. Also, I play around with tweaking games. Not so much lately— I've been working on the house—but I do make some time for it. It's my stress reliever."

"I need to find me something that relieves stress. Killing things or people isn't legal for most of the world." Heath laughed when she did. "The Wiccan inside of me? My friend, Boddy, did that. At least, I think he did. I saved his ass, and he figured he owed me. I thought he was only making sure I healed quickly by sending me to a jaguar leader. I was changed to one when it was obvious to me that my job was going to get me killed. I think he gave me a little more than I asked for." Heath told her it was enough to call out to Rebel. "She told me. Also, she said that while there is very little in me, she believes it is what makes me so good at my job. Observant and shit like that. Do you own a gun? And can you use it?"

He lifted his pant leg and showed her the ankle holster there. She was glad he was armed all the time, but she didn't care for the fact that he had to be. Harris. Paige thought she was the main reason all of them were still around. Well, more than likely all the Marshall family.

"I can fire it at targets. However, I've never used it against another person. I can if it comes to my family. Which would include you and your family. But I do have my cat, who is happy to have you in our life." She got up and looked around. "You're still healing. I can tell you that if you'd like to shift to take care of the soreness and wounds, I believe you're more than strong enough to handle it now. I'll be here if you get too weak to move around after you're healed."

Paige wasted no time in letting her cat take her. Stretching out and letting her other half feel the soil beneath her claws, she took off toward the wooded area and let her cat do whatever she wanted. It was not just a good feeling but invigorating as well.

Turning when she heard something, she let the fall leaves and dark trees cover her as she waited for whoever it was to show themselves. She was both happy and disappointed that it was James in the woods with her.

You're feeling well, I take it. She told him she'd never felt better. *I'm glad to see you up and around, to be honest with you. You've no idea how worried I've been about you and the kids. But tell me, does it have more to do with the young man that is your mate, or just in general?*

Both. And I think the kids are less stressed than you are right now. He laughed, and they both turned when Heath came into the woods as his cat. *He's fucking huge. I suppose it has something to do with him being a pureblood.*

I have no idea. But I'd not fuck with him. I'm glad he's your mate, Paige, or I think he'd eat me alive. She'd not thought of that and assured Heath that it was her brother. Heath told her that they'd met. The tension she was feeling seemed to dissipate right away. *Thank you. I'm going to head in now. You guys have fun.*

Fun? Paige didn't know how to have fun anymore, she realized. Not only that, but she couldn't for the life of her remember the last time she'd even had sex. When Heath's bigger cat rubbed his body next to hers, she did the same to him. Then she took off running again for the simple pleasure of having him chase her. Yes, she thought, this might be considered fun.

They played in the wooded area until well after dark. Both of them seemed to be exhausted, so she was glad when he laid down next to the large stream that both of them had crossed several times while they'd been out. As soon as she laid down next to him, the tug of being exhausted seemed to take her hard.

Her mind didn't rest, however. Paige had always been better at figuring out things while she slept. It was as if her mind relaxed enough that she could see things she'd not been able to before. As her mind worked its way back to the bar she and James had been in, she felt as if she could not just look around at the things she'd seen before, but she was able to look around when the real her was staring at the table in front of her. Like she was having an out-of-body experience, and she was able to see from other perspectives. Paige thought this was really freaky.

There she saw the woman they'd been there to take. The bartender was a local, one that she'd been watching for the last several weeks. There were other patrons too, all of them sitting around drinking coffee from those tiny little cups they seemed never to be without. Paige thought they hung them on a small chain around their necks so they could have a cup at any time.

Watching the doorway, the five men that had spooked the locals walked in, each wearing a thawb. The ankle-length dress-like clothing usually had long sleeves. These idiots had not just taken the sleeves off but had torn them from the thawb to be cooler in the heat, she was sure. Their keffiyeh, the headwear common to this part of the world, had been taken off as soon as they entered the little place. Their dress pants, as well as tennis shoes, marked them as something other than what they were trying to portray right away. Again, she thought they were idiots.

Harris, now that she'd gotten to know her, would never have sent anyone in that was so poorly prepared as these men were. It looked to Paige as if they'd looked up what the local clothing was like and made do. You could never make do when in situations like this one.

"Do you see her?" She looked around when the man did that seemed to be in charge. "She's supposed to be easy to spot. Someone that doesn't fit in."

Well, if that wasn't the pot calling the kettle black. When he stared openly at her and James's target, she made her way closer to the woman to see what she was doing on her phone. Messaging. Telling someone that she could see the Feds now. A chill ran up her spine when she realized the woman they'd been sent to find was helping the murderers.

"Can you read that?" She turned and looked at Heath. "I don't have any idea why I'd be here with you, but whatever she's saying in that message is much more important than what is going on. See if you can make her scroll upwards on the chat area. That way, we can see, maybe anyway, what she's saying."

Turning to their target, she whispered in her ear, and the woman did just that, scrolled to the top of the chat so that she could read not only what was said prior to what she'd read but also the beginning of the contact.

"The person she's speaking with contacted her first. He is only coming up as unknown, so I can't figure who he is by that. Funny too that they're speaking Russian. The language spoken around here to put the Feds off." Slowly the text messages began to make more sense than the last one did. "He wanted her to meet the man from the support team here. He doesn't call him by name, but I'm betting it's James."

"Good to know. So go on. Tell me what else you can read. While you're doing that, I'm going to take note of the things I can see too." She read the rest of the messages from the last two weeks. Heath was behind the bar by then and told her that there were pictures back there. Going to look at them, she could see that they were pictures of not just James but the five men that had come in last. "I'm not sure who did this, but this picture, after meeting James, is from some time ago. His hair was a great deal lighter than it is now. Also, there is the surroundings. It looks like this was taken in an airport."

"It was. They've cut out the picture of his wife. I remember this day. It was the same day Sara was murdered. Do you suppose they were supposed to murder them both that day?" Heath told her that there were no pictures of her, then asked if Paige was supposed to have been with her brother that day. "No. I mean, I knew where he was going to get the target, but I only showed up to give him the message I'd gotten. Wait. How did they know to message me about James?"

"I'm sure I couldn't tell you, but if it's not right to you, then I'd say you've every reason to be questioning it. Who would have known about you and James being related? Also, who would have been able to give him the information to go to that place for the target?" She didn't know and told Heath that. "Okay. Something that needs to be checked into. The place was blown up. I'm assuming it was taken out to keep any kind of information from getting out, right?"

"Yes." He told her what he was thinking. "Can we do that, do you think? I mean, I've never had this much…I guess you could call it ability when I think over a situation."

"It can't hurt to try. What do we have to lose?" Nothing, she told him. Making her way around the place, taking cell phones from the tables and putting them in her pockets, she also gathered what other information she could, even going so far as to take glasses from the table for some fingerprints. Heath gathered up the wallets of the Feds, as well as the rest of the men in the room. "The kitchen will need to be gone over as well."

Back there, they found a very good reason not to have eaten there. Large amounts of soup were in filthy buckets on the floor. The walls looked like a slaughterhouse. The walk-in had two bodies in it that were naked and hanging from meat hooks. The place was nasty, and she wanted out of there in the worst sort of way.

Taking one of the plastic containers that might well have held herbs, she began putting her things into it to carry more. Heath did the same thing. No women were in the place, but she found several burkas, the women's clothing for this part of the world. Head coverings as well. Taking one of the headdresses, she put it in the container as well.

By the time they were finished gathering things, Heath suggested that they take them to a place where no one would find them. Putting them into an empty building she knew hadn't been hit by the bomb that had gone off, they both made their way back to the bar and watched as an individual man came into the place, dressed as any other businessman from one of the larger cities.

When the first volley of bullets went off, she nearly ran to hide. But they didn't touch her, other than to go through her as if she wasn't there. Which, she supposed, she wasn't. The man now that she had time to pay attention, looked right at James's target and nodded once. Then he opened fire, pulling a second then third submachine gun to his front as he made short work of everyone still in the place after she and James had left.

"I know him." She looked at Heath when he spoke. "I don't know him really, but I've seen his picture. Where? I've no idea, but it'll come to me. He has a wallet, as well as a lanyard around his neck. I'm going to go and get them both before we wake up.

Because I don't know about you, but I've had enough
of this shit for two lifetimes."

Sitting up as soon as she woke, Paige realized it
was morning and that the two of them had been out
all night. Wondering if anything she'd dreamt was
true, she looked over at Heath as he sat behind her
quietly.

*This is some next-level shit that we can do, Paige.
Unless you could do this before.* She said she'd not been
able to. *Good to know. So we're mates and able to — Rebel.
We have to get Rebel to get the things we left there. Christ, I
hope they're still there. I think this would go a fucking long
way in figuring this out, don't you?*

She laughed before speaking. *I think that's an
understatement.* Shifting back to their human selves,
Paige commented on the fact that they were both
dressed. "I've never done that before. Been dressed
after shifting."

"Me either. And I left my clothing on the deck,
so I'm not sure how this happened. But I think it will
be a good thing if we're fleeing from someone and can
shift from cat to human. Maybe we can figure it out
sometime if we can change our clothing. That would
be very helpful." Paige agreed with him. "Before I
forget to ask, could you allow my family to have a
taste of your blood? That way, we'd all be able to
communicate. Also, for your brother and his family to

do the same with mine. You never know how it might be handy to know that we can contact each other."

"I'll have no trouble with it, but James might take some convincing. I'll talk to them." Heath thanked her and took her hand into his much larger one as they made their way to the house. "I'm starving. Is that normal?"

"Normal? I don't even know what that word means anymore, do you?"

They were both laughing as they entered the house. He told his sister-in-law what they'd been able to do and asked her if she'd take them to get the things they'd collected. In seconds, not only had she been able to bring the two boxes with her, but she had the clothing as well. This was some freaking fucking stuff, Paige thought.

Chapter 2

Harris was running the things that had been given to her in the database she was privy to now. Part of her mind was working on pulling prints, while the other half was trying to figure out how the fuck Heath and Paige had been able to secure this shit.

"I have a hit, sir." She looked over at the man who had been her right hand man since she'd taken over this job as director of the FBI, Dan Conklin. "The first name that popped up was an unknown, but I put the print back into the operation as you suggested. I think the better picture is what it got. Thank you. His last name is Hofer. There is only an initial for his first. A. Could be one of five that are in the system. I think if we could get Major Avery in here to have a look at the faces, she'll be able to pick the right one out."

That was another thing that had her mind boggled. Not only was Paige a USASOC, United States

Army Special Operations Command, but so was her brother. Pulling up their records had been difficult to do, but once she got them, Harris was blown away. These two had been at this a good deal longer, she thought, than anyone might have known. Forgetting for a moment what she'd been doing, she looked at the man standing there and nodded.

"Call her in and ask her to see me after she's finished in there. I have Heath working on some pictures of the person he said he might have recognized. Hopefully, he can figure it out, and we can get this shit fixed." Harris managed to pull three more prints off the teacup handles and beer bottles before Paige joined her. "Did you figure out who he was for Dan?"

"Yes, sir." Harris just glared at the other woman. "Look, you've been at this civilian shit longer than I have. It's not any easier for me to call you by your given name than it is for me to raise the fucking dead. Deal with it. Fuck. You're a pain in the ass."

"You can't call me by my first name, but you call me a pain in the ass. Something in that logic is fucked up in my way of thinking." She went back to her work, then turned back to look at Paige. "Did you hint that you're trying to be a civilian?"

"I'm not sure I can go back out there. And before you start adding up two and getting six, yes, we've discussed my sister's kids. If I would have been here, Butch would be dead too. Can you imagine killing the woman that was having your child simply because she was having a daughter? I heard that he's bitching because no one put his name on the birth certificate for the twins that Belinda was going to have. I hate people. With that, I'm not sure what sort of mother I'd be. The first thing I'd be teaching them after they could say the word fuck was how to aim properly and shoot. What sort of mother-of-the-year shit do you think I'd get for that? I'm sure the PTA or whatever the fuck they go by now would be just as thrilled as punch for me to do that."

"More than likely, our kids will be able to take out a shooter before the police arrive. But I understand. When I pop this kid, I have a lot of family that can show me the ropes. You'll be raising those little girls after them being abused badly and never hearing a kind word from a male figure. I don't envy you at all." Paige sat—well, more like flopped—into the chair across from her. "What else is bothering you? Something is eating you. Tell me, and let me make fun of you before I fix it for you."

"This shit that I can do. I've never been able to— I could go over the scene in my mind later, usually at bedtime, but Heath and I could go around that pub and take shit while we were having an out-of-body experience. Doesn't that just sound like insanity with a capital I?" Harris asked her what Rebel had said about it as she put in the information on one of the identifications they'd brought back for her. "She was no fucking help. Her suggestion was to tell me that this was only the tip of the pile of shit in what we'd be able to do with this. That didn't help me or Heath. But instead of walking away like he did, I got up in her face. Remind me never to do that again."

"What did she do to you?" Harris didn't think Paige was going to answer, but when she did, Harris had to stand up. She was laughing so hard. "She actually turned you into a carrot. Oh my goodness, I wish I had seen that."

"I could see her as she showed me that she could take a bite out of me while I was in that form. Not only that, but she threatened me by saying she'd turn me into a flea and put me on Rodney's back. She's evil." Harris was still laughing when Heath joined them in her office. "Did you find him?"

"I did." He didn't look happy with his find, and she put out her hand for the picture that he had in his hand. "Before I give this to you, I have two questions for you. How many of the prints have you been able to find? Any of them from people along your food chain?"

Her heart started beating faster as she nodded.

"Am I going to be pissy about this, or are you yanking my chain, Heath? I've been doing really well with the new president, and I'm enjoying working for him. Am I going to have to kill him?"

"Not him, no. But someone close to him." He handed her the picture, and she could only stare at one of the new people in office. "I don't know him well enough to have remembered who he was at the time, but as I was going through the pictures you gave me, I decided to take a break and look into the news feed, just clearing my mind, when this showed up first thing. I'm not mistaken about who he is, Harris. That was the man that opened fire on the pub we were all in."

Covering the picture when she heard someone coming toward them, Harris smiled at one of her men as he asked if she needed anything else before he headed back to the office. After telling him no, that she wasn't having any luck on anything she had, he turned and left. It wasn't until she heard the crunch of tires on the driveway that she pulled out the picture Heath had printed off to get a closer look.

"Do you suppose he was in with the other three and was simply overlooked?" Harris didn't answer Heath but read the headline of the article he'd gotten the picture from. "He knows you and us, Harris. He knows not only where we live, but he's been here several times as you were being set up with the new computers."

"You're not helping, Heath." Paige got up and moved to her side of the table. "Holy fuck balls. All right, I'm officially freaked the fuck out. How? Not only how was he able to get in and out of the country without anyone saying anything, but where the fuck did he get the balls to try and kill everyone?"

"Do you know this man?" She pointed to the man on the right of the one that Heath had identified. Heath said he didn't know him. She posed the same question to Paige. "This man here, next to the shooter, do you think your brother might know who he is? I'm going to ask you something that I don't want you to be pissy about, Paige, but do you trust that your bother had nothing to do with this?"

"On my life, I trust him." That was good enough for her, but when James came into the office, she knew Paige had called him. "We have a picture we want you to look at. I want you to tell us truthfully, James. Do you not only know him but do you work for him too?"

James was smiling when he came into the room, and Harris could see that whatever he was thinking now had taken all that happiness away and a good deal more. As he sat down on the chair that Paige had been sitting in, he continued to stare at the man in the picture. It wasn't until Paige hit her brother in the back of the head that he looked at Harris and his sister.

"I saw him in the doorway. Or, at the time, I thought I saw him standing there. My mind, I thought at the time, was playing tricks on me. You know, with all the shit that was going down?" Harris nodded; Paige hit her brother again. "I'm working up to it, damn it. Back the fuck off. Do you know who this is, Paige? He signs my fucking paychecks. Not yours, of course, but he does mine."

"Wait. Why doesn't he sign your paychecks?" Harris was glad that someone else had asked the question when Heath did. Paige surely wasn't doing this for fucking free, was she? "Are you saying they pay you in other forms of payroll?"

"Cash." Paige looked at her when dawning hit her. "Yes, so there is no trace of me anywhere in anyone's system. I work for all the branches. Not just the CIA, but the FBI, FDA — If it has to do with some sort of government entity, then you can bet your sweet ass that I'm working for them."

"How is that possible?" Harris felt sorry for Heath. He wasn't military, nor did he have a great deal to do with all the shit that she was into. But Paige opened up a whole new set of rules when she worked. Harris would bet anything that there were no rules when she was out working. "How the hell do you carry around the money they pay you? I'm not mad. Please don't think that. But my head isn't taking this well. Just…I don't know. Just give me a minute to digest this."

"I have money stashed all over the world." Heath simply nodded when Paige began explaining things to him. Harris wanted to tell her to hold off, but she wasn't anyone that Harris wanted to fuck around with. At least not until she figured out just what Paige was capable of. "I know you're wealthy—your entire family is. But I have this, and I'm going to put it in with the rest of the money that is already here. I've already spoken to Rebel, and she and I are going to go popping around the world to pick it all up. Knowing that I can get in and out quickly will make it—"

"You're not going alone." They all turned to James when he spoke. "Paige. Be reasonable, please. Do you see who this man is? He's the fucking chief of staff. To the fucking president of the United States. No, I forbid you going alone."

"In the event that it might have skipped something in that tiny Neanderthal mind of yours, I'm a fucking grown assed woman who carries a gun everywhere she goes. Not to mention I'm an immortal, have a mate of my own, and I didn't fucking say I was going alone, now did I? You fucking prick. No, not a prick, but a fucking asshole of a prick that is lucky I'm in a good mood, or I'd tear that fucking appendage off you that you're so proud of when there are women around and serve it up kebab style with skewers all the way through it. Have you got it that I don't give two good shits what you think I should do at any given time in my life?" He said he got it. More like he mumbled it. "You had better speak up, James, or so help me I'm going to go all pissed off on you."

"I said I was sorry. Christ, you're a mean person." James looked at Heath. "Do you care that she's going to go out there with another woman in this family? And they're all alone?"

"First of all, I know for a fact that she's better trained in combat than I'd ever be. So if she thinks she'll be safe doing this, then I trust her to be safe. Secondly, have you met your sister and Rebel? Not only is Rebel the most magical person I've ever seen, but she's also smart and savvy. Your sister is kick assed enough that she was willing, and I'm sure quite able, to do to you just what she said she'd do and not be bothered by the fallout at all. I've no doubt that she would hurt me too if I thought to tell her — no forbid her to do something she is going to do anyway no matter what anyone has to say about it." Heath stood up and stretched, letting a little of his cat go so that the other man could see that he was much larger than he was. "And here is the thing you should be thinking about more than if your sister, my mate, will be safe. I will tear you apart while you're still breathing, and no one, not even with the best equipment around, will find you if you ever speak to her like that again. Do I make myself clear?"

"Yes, sir." Heath put out his hand to Paige, and she took it. The two of them left the room without a word. Harris looked at James. He was pale and a little frightened looking. "I don't know, but I think I'm more afraid of Heath than I am Paige. He's the calm sort of stab you in the chest sort of man, isn't he?"

"I'd say that's a fair estimation. To be honest with you, James. I was a little frightened for you myself. You really fucked up." He nodded and asked her what he could do to remedy this. "Get your head out of your ass, and don't piss anyone else off. I'd say, immortal or not, you will live longer if you think before speaking."

"I think you might be right on that." She only nodded. "All right. I'm going to see what I can do in the other office you have. I'm sure there are some things I can do that will have me out of sight for a few hours."

"Good thinking."

When he left her, she sat there thinking about what was going on at the White House again.

Another ass trying to fuck things up. While she didn't know what his plan was, Conley Parker was going to disappear soon if anything harmed anyone in this family.

For the rest of the afternoon, Harris worked on the information from the prints and the DNA on the items she had. Dan brought her a glass of juice, telling her it was from Rebel, and Harris enjoyed having some of the wonderful liquid when she was thirsty. Dan also showed her the chart he was working on.

"It's the list of people of the White House. Their jobs, as well as anyone that I could find that works directly with them. The names with the blue mark by them are people we have some indicator that they have ties with Conley. The rest of the names, a lot of them are casual workers that he employees when he needs an extra hand." She asked him if he'd been able to find anyone that could vouch for him being in his office when the shit hit the fan. "Not yet. However, he's not married, has no children, and lives alone. There isn't much in the way of staff either. Actually, just one person—a cook that doubles as a housekeeper. I'm digging into her life as we speak."

"Good job. On that and this chart." She looked it over and was startled by how few people worked directly with the speaker. "According to this, he has no contact with the sitting president. Can you see if he did the previous one? I'd like to say I would know that, but to be honest, nothing would surprise me much anymore."

"He sends emails or text messages to him. Also—and I find this odd—he doesn't eat anything that is brought in or served in the cafeteria, nor does he drink the water. Not unless it's something he brought in that morning. There is no coffee pot in his office, nor a computer that I can find." She looked at Dan. "There is something else too. I'm not even sure you're going to find it odd—as you said, with all the other crap going on—but I can't find any social media accounts linked to him. Nor does he seem to own a television. Not even a small one in his bedroom."

"That is very strange. Do you know if he has Internet access at home?" He said he'd not thought to look. "Do that. And if he does, then we can only assume he has something that requires it. Also, see if there is a bomb shelter on the property. You might have to go back a ways on that search."

When Dan left her, she looked at the picture that Heath had given her and the chart that Dan had made. Something wasn't clicking. Not only that, but the things that should have been easy weren't. This would require her to do some heavy research. But for now, she needed a nap. The baby seemed to be sucking all her energy out of her, and he wasn't even born yet.

~*~

Paige had the longitude and the latitude on each place she had money. Rebel said that would make it as simple as going there and returning since they didn't have to walk around to get what she was after. That was good. The less time she spent in some of the places, the better. As soon as the first three pick-ups were finished, she was waiting for the other shoe to drop on her head.

Each time they popped back to the house she was living in with Heath, he was there waiting with a kiss for her and a glass of juice for Rebel. There was also not only a large crate for her to put the money in but a table for the things she might have collected when she'd been in that part of the world.

Mostly it was paintings. An occasional bottle of something like herbs that she'd fallen in love with. All the things brought back memories of the trip there, as well as a memory of whatever she'd been doing. After giving a brief statement about what she'd done there to Heath, he would write it down in a notebook. She hadn't any idea why he thought that was important, but right now, she just wanted to collect the stuff and be done.

They had no trouble at all with the stops up until the point where she wanted to find Boddy.

Pausing for a few minutes in Ireland, she asked Rebel if she could find him. The place they were in now was where he'd healed her, as well as sent her to a shadow to be changed.

"He's close by if you'd like to speak to him. It would be easy enough for me to summon him to us. But why does it matter to you?" She looked around the countryside and turned back to Rebel. "Do you want me to bring him to you? Or better yet, I can see what he's thinking, and we can go from there. Either way is no sweat off my balls."

"I do believe you have a set of them. Mythically speaking, of course. Tell me if you can find why he gave me the bit of extra when he sent me to the wolf." Rebel said she had it. "Just like that? All you had to do was peek into his head for that little bit of time? Christ, you're good."

"He didn't want you to die if the changing went wrong. Not only that, but he also knows you're making sure he has money in his account each month, and he is only alive because of something you taught him. May I ask what that might have been?" She told the other women. "I like that. Teaching him how to tell the difference between poison plants and not poison afforded him the ability to not only take care of any unwanted foes but for him to build them up in his system too. Smart girl."

The rest of the pick-ups were just as uneventful. As they were standing in Heath's house—their house, she supposed—Paige asked Rebel if she owed her anything other than the endless supply of gratitude and friendship.

"Make Heath happy. Be my friend. That's all I need, really." Paige hugged her. "That helps too. Tomorrow we're having a girl's luncheon with Bella. She's going to scope out some of the better nursing homes for her dad, and we thought we'd cheer her up when she's finished. Have you met him? Fletcher, I mean?"

"No. When I went to their home, Dean and Bella's, they told me Fletcher was having a bad day. The only thing I'm to understand that works in calming him is the baby, Dru. But they're worried he might hurt Dru too." Rebel told her that Grandda helped a great deal, but he was a little too old to be trying to get away from Fletcher when he was upset. "I can't imagine it's very easy on any of you guys in helping her with him. Grace told me that all of you help out when you can. That's a real family there."

They were seated at the table when Heath joined them. There was fruit and veggies on a tray with some dip. Paige got up to get some cheese but forgot the crackers. Rebel took care that they had some with her magic.

"I guess you've figured out all this mess by now. The magic, I mean. Sometimes, here lately, when I do something, I just chalk it up to new shit I have to learn." Rebel told her she could help her with that. "You mean take it away? No thanks. I'm beginning to see its usefulness now."

"I meant I can give you a better understanding of what you have. I'd never take the magic away from you. I would to someone abusing the right to use it, but not you. I have, just so you know, tweaked the bit that your niece and nephews have. Just to give them a little extra while they're going to school and such." Rebel asked her if she was happy here. "This is a far change from what you're used to, I'd think. Sleeping when you got the chance, as well as eating whatever you could find."

"I do love it here." Paige looked at Heath. "He's made me feel very welcome here. All of you have, as a matter of fact. It wouldn't bother me at all if I were to never have to go out of the country again. But I know that there is no point in wishing that. I have a job to do, and I love it. I feel as if I'm making a difference."

"You are. In my life, as well as the countries." Heath kissed the back of her hand and stood up. "I have to get into town. The gazebo has been taken apart, and the new wood has arrived. Grandda sold all the wood he was keeping back for large donations, and now he's looking to see if he can get names put into the wood that the gazebo is going to be made with. The entire town is coming together with this thing." After a kiss, he left her with Rebel.

"May I ask you how Sara was killed?" Paige didn't want to bring her up now, but Rebel and the rest of them deserved to know what had gone down that day. "If you'd rather not say, I can understand."

"No, it's not that. I didn't even like Sara. Not all that much. I guess I got used to her over time, but we were never really on any kind of friendly terms. She wasn't a good mom either. I don't think that she ever loved my brother. Also, she could be a bit pig headed about shit. Like not stupidly so, but she would argue for the sake of arguing. The day she was killed, I was just coming home from a month long job. She'd told the kids we were going to have a nice cookout, and she wanted to go get steaks. Seems innocent enough, right?" Rebel nodded. "When I got off the transport, she was in the lobby of the place waiting for me, waving at me like she'd not seen me in years rather than the month. I was startled at first, then pissed. There isn't any better way to tell that you're related to someone than to pick them up at the airport. And there she was, waving like she was my best friend. The three men came out of nowhere. I mean, like they were just there. I killed two of them after they'd filled

Sara full of holes, and the third guy was killed when he ran from me into the oncoming traffic at the airport. Sara was dead before she hit the floor. Forty bullet holes, and most of them in her chest. It pissed me off more because she'd not taken any kind of precautions with being out there. Not a vest or even a gun on her person." Rebel asked why they were all pretending that she was still alive. "So that no one would know that it was his wife that was dead. Or that someone had killed her. Had it come out that Sara had been murdered, where and when, then connecting the dots to either of us would have been only a small thing to do. Understand?"

"What happened then?" She said she'd had to contact James and tell him that his wife was an idiot and had gotten herself killed. "I don't know why I think this, but you were a little less harsh about it, right?"

"No. I wasn't. She knew better. Her and James had been married for a while and had their kids by then. James said she'd gotten domesticated while living in the States, and he was pissed too. Neither of us could go to the funeral because it was more than likely a trap. So he packed up his family and made his home in Germany. No one claimed responsibility for killing her, and as far as I know, because of the lies we've all been saying, everyone thinks Sara is alive and well. That's why Beth pretends to be her when he has a function he needs to attend. All we need to do is call our number, talk to or about Sara, and Beth knows she has to step into the role. It's been our code since her mother died. It's all a cover. I think he hammers home to the children daily about being on point all the time. Beth is beginning to revolt at all the stress, and Billy just wants to have some fun with the other kids around. Jamie, he's all right with everything, but I think because he lost his mom at such a young age, he's terrified of losing someone else." Rebel asked if he might need to see someone about it. "I think he is, as a matter of fact. Sheppard is hanging around with him and Billy. That man could charm the nuts off a bull the way he's working himself into their lives. He's asked me if he could take them with him when he takes his trip. I think it would be good for them, but it's not up to me."

"No, I can see that." Rebel stood up, saying that she needed to get home. "Let me know if you need anything else, Paige. I've enjoyed this time with you. Let me know what you decide on tomorrow. I think Bella is going to need us to rally around her when she has her dad put in a nursing home."

After she left, Paige realized she was the only one in the house. Normally that didn't bother her—she always had something to do. Going to the kitchen, she was wondering if she should start dinner when Beth came to the back door. She was sporting a black eye and a bloodied lip. Paige smiled at her when she showed her that she had busted knuckles as well. Not freaking out was the main reason she'd bet that she came to her to clean up rather than finding her dad.

"Two guys on the wrestling team thought it would be hilarious to tease me about my boots. Why? Who gives a crap what I put on my feet so long as I'm not bothering them?" Paige wisely said nothing. "Anyway, they started calling me a shit kicker. Even I know that was lame, but I'd had a crappy morning, and I didn't get to take it out on the punching bag. So I took it out on them."

"Are they hurt?" She waved her hand back and forth as if she were saying so-so. "Did you get into trouble at school? Am I going to have to go there and knock someone around for you?"

"Nah. I did myself proud. I told them they were harassing me and that I retaliated. I didn't think that was going to go over well when the principal asked me who had helped me. Of course, he didn't believe it was just me, and I asked him if he wanted me to show him how I'd done it all on my own. The idiot said yes." Beth was laughing then. "I doubt very much that he'll be asking me for any other display about how I defend myself. Nor if I had any help. He has a broken nose and a cut lip, and he's going to need a wrist brace for a while if I didn't actually break it."

"So how come you're beat to shit? Did he fight back?" Beth grinned and hurt her lip in the process. "This is going to be good, isn't it?"

"Very good. When the demo was over, I was standing there when someone touched me on the shoulder. I hadn't any idea who it was, but I was still in defense mode. After socking the gym teacher in the face, I was taken down by not one or two but five of the other teachers. They got a little zealous when I was trying to get up and hit me. By accident, they said." Beth snorted. "Accident, my ass. I think they were getting in a good one because I'd hurt the principal as well as the gym teacher."

She was still laughing about it when she and Beth decided to go into town for some dinner. Jamie was going to meet them there, and Billy was hanging out with Heath at the gazebo. They were just getting their dinner when not only did Heath join them, but Sheppard did as well. She was beginning to really love this family.

Chapter 3

Heath was helping Bella find a place for her dad to live out the rest of his days. Grandda planned to come with her, but he'd been called into work at the last minute, so Heath had been asked to go. Since Paige was working with Harris, he said he'd love to help her out. Dru came along, too, as he was about the only thing that would get Fletcher into and out of a car when they had to travel.

In the few months since the man had come to live around them, Heath could see how much he'd deteriorated. Not only was his short-term memory terrible, but he had trouble remembering himself at times. Or even Bella. But he'd light right up when he saw Dru and would hold him gently and talk to him. But that, too, was coming to an end. The talk was mostly nonsense stuff now, but he'd been calm while he was around the baby. This outing was going to be hard on him, as well as Bella.

The first two places they went to, Fletcher refused to go much further than the front desk. He said they stank. The place did actually stink, but he was surprised that Fletcher could smell it. They were headed to their fourth place when Dru had had enough of being in the car seat, and they went through a drive-thru and found them a place to eat that had a picnic table. Everyone seemed to enjoy that. Fletcher looked at him and seemed so sad. He spoke to him as Bella got Dru's bottle set up.

"I'm not doing well, am I, Heath?" He told him that was why they were out today. The doctor had told them, no matter what, don't ever lie to him, even if they thought it would be better. "I knew this day was coming, but I thought I'd have a bit more time."

"I think Bella did as well." He nodded and looked at his daughter while Heath continued. "What would you like in a place to stay, Fletcher? I mean, your own room, of course. Some of the things from your home. But what would you like to have in a place to stay?"

"No television in my room." He had noticed that the older man didn't care for watching much television. The doctor said it made him anxious, and that was more than likely the reason for it. "You think your grandpa would come to visit me?"

"He said he'd be coming around for a rematch all the time. Grandda also said he'd be sneaking you in something good to eat. Some pie, if I don't miss my bet."

Fletcher nodded and took Dru when Bella handed him to her dad. "This little man here, he'll not remember all the time we've spent together. Having our little talks about life. I know I have another child, but it eludes me when I try and think of some of the things we might have done. All the things that I wish I'd been able to do with…with…. I can't remember his name anymore."

"Dru, Dad. Your grandson is Dru, and your son was Hunter Booth." When he seemed satisfied with the help, he spoke to Dru again. Bella turned to Heath. *I'm so glad he doesn't ask more than that. He never does, but I'm not sure what I'd say to him if he were to ask me where Hunter is.*

I'm thinking he only remembers he has a son and nothing more. I believe Hunter was forever hurting your dad, and he only needs a name to refer to him as such. Bella nodded, and he spoke aloud again. "This next place? What do you know about it?"

"It's privately owned and operated. People like Dad are the only kind of people in the place, and they've trained their staff well. Their ratings are very high on how to deal with a combative patient.

Harris has dug deep into their records and can't find anything wrong with it. And you know as well as I do that she dug really hard." He asked her why they were seeing this one last. "It's the furthest away from our house. It's only forty-five minutes, but I wanted him to be closer. Silly, I know. The doctor said he'd know me less and less as he goes on."

"I understand, Bella. You've missed a lot of time with him, and you're not able to make up for it." While she cried on his shoulder, he held her. Heath loved the women of his family and was happy he could be there for them when they needed a hug or a shoulder to cry on. "I have you, honey. Never forget that I'm always here for you."

Bella had had a terrible life up until meeting his brother and falling in love. Not only that, but she'd been dealing with the fallout from her brother and the things he'd been up to. Hunter had been a murderer and a con. He'd pitted his sister and dad against one another for a long time before Bella had been able to slip in and see her dad once. It had made all the difference in the world for them both. That was when she'd found out that Hunter had been hurting their dad and stealing from him. Heath was glad he was out of all their lives now.

The trip to the next place was much nicer. Dru and Fletcher were taking a nap, and he and Bella talked about the gazebo that was being built. As soon as they pulled into the parking lot, Fletcher woke up and got out of the car. It was the first time he'd done that on any trip, but especially the one they were on today.

The manager and owner of Hallow Lane, Tanner Lipswitch, came out to meet them after Fletcher had gone inside. He told Bella that her dad was talking to the staff already and making himself known to the others. This was the first time he'd done that as well.

Tanner showed them around the entire place. Not only where the residents lived in their little apartments, but the kitchen, as well as the room where they held classes one on one with some of the people there. He never once called them patients and frowned at the word when he heard it. So far, Heath was really liking this place.

"Mr. Lipswitch, Mr. Booth is in the reading room. I think you all should come and see what he's up to." Afraid of what he might be doing, he and Bella raced ahead to see if they could help in getting her dad taken care of. "He's been in here for the last twenty minutes. I think that old piano hasn't been played since Mr. April died some months past."

Fletcher *was* playing the piano and was encouraging the others to sing to the hymns that he was pounding out on the thing. He seemed to be enjoying himself but stopped when he saw the two of them.

"Hello. You have a baby." Fletcher was gone again, and this shy man was there to talk to his daughter and grandson without any knowledge of who they were to him. "Would you mind if I showed him off to my friends? Oh my, he's a cute little guy, isn't he?"

Fletcher never allowed any of the people there to hold Dru, but he did let them touch him. Dru was awake now and seemed to be having as much fun as his grandda was. When Fletcher sat back down at the piano again, he played one handed some tunes that Heath remembered from his own childhood.

Bella left him sitting in the room with Fletcher while she went with Tanner to see about her dad's room. There could be no better testimony than this for the man to be comfortable living here. He watched the older man showing off the grandson that he didn't remember right now and shed a few tears.

Heath loved Fletcher. He'd been a good man when he could and apologetic when he became combative. Not that he ever meant to harm anyone, but he knew that Dean had gotten a couple of black eyes from him and was even shot by Fletcher once when he was in a delirious state. But never once had anyone, including Dean, ever hurt Fletcher with any other intention but to keep him safe.

I have a question for you. Heath laughed and asked Shep what he could possibly want with his baby brother. *You'd be surprised. I need something to do. I know I have all these projects going on, but I need something more. I guess I need something to get me away from being on what seems like several hundred projects at one time.*

What did you have in mind? I'm game for just about anything. Actually, I have a couple of games in the works, but those are coming along nicely. Shep asked him where he was. *With Bella and Fletcher. I think she's settled on this place we're at now, Hallow Lane. Fletcher is acting like he's found a place he can be comfortable in forever. Bella is filling out the paperwork now. I'm thinking of seeing if she'd like to have dinner with me on the way home.*

I think the women are going to be taking her to a late lunch to cheer her up. Heath told Shep she'd more than likely enjoy that more anyway. *Doubtful. You'll hold her hand when she's upset. The others will bully her into being in a better mood. You remember them, don't you?*

They were both laughing when Dru was brought back to him. Fletcher thanked him several times for allowing him to show the baby off and walked back to the piano and the crowd that had gathered around him in the few minutes he'd had the baby. It hurt Heath so badly that the man had no idea who he'd been holding and how much he loved him.

Asking his brother if he wanted to have dinner with him, he said he'd ask the others if they wanted to join them as well. Heath was all for that. But he also wanted to get Paige alone sometime and see if they could talk. There were plenty of conversations they'd started, but nothing was settled. He also wanted to make love to her in the worst sort of way.

After they left, leaving Fletcher there as he wanted, Heath dropped Bella off at the restaurant where the other women were meeting her. He almost felt sorry for her. But he also knew that she could take care of herself as much as the rest of them could. Before heading to the restaurant he and his brothers had decided on, having plenty of time now, Heath went to the jewelry store to find a special gift for Paige. A wedding band came to mind, as well as an engagement ring.

Tomorrow he was going to go and have another talk with Belinda's little girls. Mary, the older of her daughters at five, was doing much better around the hospital staff, but Angel, almost four, was a harder nut to crack. Even being the youngest of the two of them, Angel was very cautious about who she would allow close to her and even more so who could touch her. They were also going to bring the twins home with them. He hoped.

They would only be in their care temporarily. Their father was in jail for murder and two accounts of attempted murder, child abuse, and a long list of other crimes. But until he was convicted of them, he still was the one that could make decisions about the kids. Every day they were all afraid he'd say something that would jeopardize the lives of the little girls. He only wanted his son, it appeared. Paige and he were going to work on the assumption that they'd be their aunt and uncle until such time they'd be able to adopt them to give them a much better life. Again, he hoped so.

The ring he picked out was, he thought, a perfect match to Paige's eyes. Hers were a deep sapphire blue, and the ring held a large gem of the same name with a white and pink starburst in the middle of it. The band that went with it was plain, but only for the reason that there were no gems on it. It was polished to a high sheen and would look wonderful on her finger. He bought them both, as well as a pair of earrings that were simply diamonds in a lovely setting.

When he met up with his brothers, he was glad that not only had James and his boys come along with them but Grandda too. Beth was with the women, Heath was told. The boys were shy — for about ten seconds, then they joined the others in laughter and fun.

The restaurant wasn't all that busy for a Tuesday early evening, so they took their time in getting drinks and appetizers. By the time they had ordered their dinner, everyone was talking over each other and laughing. He was glad to see that even James was having a good time.

~*~

It had been advised to them both that Heath do most of the talking to her nieces. They needed to get used to him being around them all the time, and they were going to also be able to introduce them to their younger siblings. If all that went well, they could take all four of them home today and start being a family.

Paige looked over at Heath. "Why are you so calm about all this? I'd think you'd be a nervous wreck. I certainly am." He told her he was nervous but was hiding it well. "I guess kids can smell fear. I've heard that in so many countries where I've been that I think it might be true. I don't know these children any more than I do my brother's kids. I think that's sad."

"No. It's not sad if you plan to remedy it. We'll be good for all seven of them once things start to settle down around us. The babies have no preconceived notions about how we might hurt them. They've been shot and beaten up too, even before being born, Rodney told us, but we'll love them and care for them. Mary and Angel are going to need us to take things slowly, and we can do that. Speaking of which, have you found out any more information on the shooting that you and your brother were in?" She told him she'd not, but Harris wasn't going to let it go. "Do you want her to? I mean, she won't, but she can not keep you in the loop if you'd like."

"No. I mean, it's not that." She looked at Heath. "I want a life with you. I want to raise the kids, so they don't have to worry about one of us being there for them when they need us. I know you'd be there, along with your brothers, but I want to be there for skinned knees and first times. Bike riding. Swimming. Shit like that."

They both laughed but sobered up when the girls came down the hall toward them. Heath got down on his knees right away. She did then, too and looked into their faces. Mary, bolder than her little sister, stared right back at her. Angel looked at the ragged doll she was holding.

"My name is Heath Marshall. I'm sure you guys know your aunt Paige." Mary nodded, then bumped her sister when she didn't do anything. "It's all right if you want to be shy around us. You don't know us any more than we know you. That's what we're here for today. To get to know each other."

"My dad killed my momma and my sister." Paige wanted to say something but was startled by the hatred in Mary's voice. "You gonna beat us to death too?"

"No!" She looked at Heath when he took her hand into hers after shouting at Mary. "I'm sorry. No. We'd never do anything like that. But you don't just have another sister, Mary, but you have a brother too. They're both fine. Would you like to see them?"

She wanted to. Paige could see the longing in her eyes. Angel was all for it right now and even allowed Heath to pick her up. When he put out his hand for Mary to take, she stared at it for a long time before she took Paige's hand into hers. Heath went on like it didn't hurt him as much as she could see it did by his face.

"We've been in to see the babies a couple of times. But since they had such a hard time in being born, they had to stay here until you guys were ready to go too." Setting Angel on the gurney that had been brought into this room for them to use, Heath asked Mary if he could lift her up to the same place. When she shook her head no, he got down on his knees again to talk to her. "I know you've been hurt, honey. The doctor told us of all the cuts and bruises she found when she cared for you. She also told us that you cried at night instead of sleeping. You have no idea how much I'd like to make everything better for you. I'm not going to be a perfect man. I doubt there is anyone that is perfect when it comes to raising children. But you can count on me doing my very best for you and your sisters and brother. Forever. Paige and I have a lovely home that we'd like for you to stay with us in. You can have your own room if you wish. We'll go on vacations and shopping trips together. Me? Well, I'll try and enjoy shopping with you guys."

He smiled at her. Then he looked up at her, and Paige knew in that moment that Heath was going to be the perfect man for her and the children. He was kind. Romantic. Strong and compassionate. When needed, he could be a shoulder to sob on, as well as the first person you'd want to call on when things got rough. Kissing him on the mouth, she turned and smiled at Mary and Angel.

"I think we need to see the others, don't you? I'm as excited as I can be to take the four of you home and get used to each other. The other afternoon, Grandda was—my goodness, girls, you have a great grandda. He's a special kind of man. You'll love him as much as we do." She made her hasty exit to give herself a few seconds and to ring to have the twins brought in.

Are you all right? She told Heath what she'd been thinking. *I love you too, my heart. And as soon as we can arrange it, I'd like to show you just how much I love that pretty body of yours as well. All the flirtation has made me a very hard man.*

You're a goof. But she liked that he wanted her as much as she did him. *We're going at this all ass backwards, don't you think? A home—check. Family— check. Married—nope. We need to get this all finished up so that I can sleep an entire night without wondering what you're doing in your bedroom at night.*

We have plenty of time, but I think you're right. Making love to you would take a great deal of pressure off my mind and body. He told her that the babies had arrived. *Take your time, Paige. This is a very emotional time for all six of us.*

Six? Yes, she supposed they were a family of six. Going out into the room that had been set up for them, she heard Angel ask if her brother was going to go away. She asked too if they were going to be sent away.

"Nope. You're all four mine and Paige's now. We'll have such fun. I've been talking to my grandda, and he is so excited to have pretty little girls around to talk to. He's a big talker, so you know. Also, two of my brothers are going to have babies too. Well, their wives are." He was unwrapping George when she got to the little gurney. "I want to look him over, don't you? And your sister. We named them Emma for your new sister and George for your new brother. What do you think of that?"

"Emma was my mom's middle name." Heath told Angel she was right. "I don't know any George people."

"It was my grandda's name. He would have been your great grandda, too, had he lived to see you." Paige unwrapped Emma. "They wrap them up like a burrito or something, don't you think? I'd hate to sleep all wrapped up like this."

The girls giggled, and Paige thought that was the best sound she'd heard in all her life. After laying Emma next to her brother, she could see that they were beautiful. Their sisters touched them gently, and Mary kept playing with Emma's hair. It was the brightest shade of blonde she'd ever seen.

"When I was a little girl, my hair was that color. I remember other kids making fun of me because of the color, and it being so curly too." She looked at Mary. "Yours is curly as well. You got that from your momma. Both of you look so much like her that it's like having her here with us."

"When my daddy would be in his mean mood, Momma would hide us in the dryer. She didn't think he'd be wanting to do any laundry, so it was a good place for us to hide." Paige looked at Heath as Mary spoke, thinking of all the dangers hiding a kid in a dryer posed. "It didn't work no ways. So one day, with our help, she took the guts out of it and then cut some big old holes in the back of it so we'd be able to breathe. We even had us some little chairs in there so we'd have something to sit on other than the floor."

"We couldn't have no light in there." Heath asked Angel why, both of them knowing why. "He'd see the shine of it, Momma told us. The water she had in there was warm, but it was better than nothing, she told us. No snacks, though. Momma was sure he'd smell them if there was something he wasn't getting. I don't ever wanna go back to him."

"You won't. That is a promise I will make to you. You'll never have to hide in dryers or go without again so long as I have breath in my body." Heath turned to her then. "You either. You are, along with these four, my number one priority from now on. I will protect you as best I can and love you with all that I am."

"Mr. Heath, I'd like to go home with you and Aunt Paige." Paige had to work hard to pull her gaze from Heath. When she was finally able to turn to the older girls, she noticed something she'd not before. They had on clothing that was too large for them. No socks nor shoes. The babies, she'd bet, had even less than they did for things to wear. This was something she'd bet never occurred to Heath either.

"How about we go do just a little bit of shopping? Mostly to get sizes, I think. Then we can order online things that you'll need and go from there. But clothing is something that I think you all need." Mary looked suspicious, but Angel was all for it. "You're going to need coats and gloves before too long and boots. I don't think I own a pair of boots but for the army issues. Then we'll get us some much deserved lunch. Pizzas? Or burgers?"

The hospital set them up with diapers and diaper bags for the babies. Both the girls were underweight, so they needed to be in a car seat as well. Paige didn't have any idea how they were going to get them all four in car seats in the back of Heath's car when they left there. But she'd sit in the trunk of the sucker if that meant they could all go home today.

The larger SUV pulled up just as they were headed out the door. Heath said that Harris had told him he'd need bigger anyway, so she took care of it. He also told her that there was another one at home for her.

It wouldn't do a bit of good to tell anyone that she would have done this. They were the best family for taking care of things just before you realized you needed it. The car seats gave them a bit of trouble, but once Heath figured it out on the first one, the other three were as simple as buckling in the children. As they were getting things set up in the car, Heath found two large bags in the back with the girls' names on them.

"Here, read this note."

As he handed the girls their bags, Paige felt tears fill her eyes. They were the best family in the world. "I didn't think the girls would have much of their own. And I don't want to even think about what sort of things they'd have to see going back to that house. So I got them some pretty clothing for their first outing with you guys. The nursing staff was more than helpful in getting the sizes for me." Paige helped Mary put on her dress, which was a perfect fit as she read the rest of the note from Harris. "The rest of us have gone to the house this morning to get things squared away there. We put bunk beds in each of their rooms until you guys figure out if they'll sleep alone or not. I'm so very proud to call you my sister, Paige. You're doing a tremendous thing with these little babies, and I hope you know that if you need anything, we're all there for you."

By the time the girls were dressed in their new clothing, including new underwear that had princesses on them, they were ready for some lunch. None of the children had ever eaten out before, and they were nervous. So she sat at the table with the children while Heath ordered. Angel helped him by standing close to him and glared at anyone that got too close to her Mr. Heath. This might be the best thing she'd ever done, Paige thought. Having a family outing.

The nuggets were a hit, as Heath thought they'd be. There were hamburgers for them too, as well as not just french fries, but onion rings and something called chicken fries. Paige was impressed that Heath got them to at least try the different things, and it was a unanimous vote that no one cared for the onion rings. Chocolate milk was a big hit, along with the white. Angel claimed that she'd never had such a good lunch in her entire life, and they all had a good laugh about that.

As they were cleaning up their mess, the babies sleeping through it all, she could see that there'd be no shopping today. Mary was nearly asleep sitting up, and Angel was trying her best to keep her eyes open as well. After getting them buckled in the car seats again, both of them were asleep and smiling. She stared at them as Heath put the diaper bags in the back end again.

"They must trust us." She asked him why he'd think that. "I doubt very much either of them slept very well in the hospital. Nor at home, for that matter. Always being on the lookout for some harm to come to them. They were either very exhausted being just children, or they trusted us enough to let their guard down. I'm going to go with the latter so I can feel good about today."

"I will too."

The drive home was quiet. As soon as they pulled into the driveway, they could see that nap time was over for all of them. The entire Marshall family and the extended families were there with not just food but gifts as well. Again, Paige thought, she couldn't have attached herself to a better family if she'd tried.

Grandda, as she was told to call him, was as happy as she'd ever seen him. He and Beth had their heads together a great deal, and she knew it was because of the cruise they were going on with Jamie. Billy wasn't going to go on this trip, as he was still a little too young to be without his parent. But they were going to have a good time with him, so he was as excited as the others were.

Holding Emma while giving her a bottle, she watched Mary as she kept an eye on her. It didn't bother her, but she wanted to ask her what she wanted to make her say something. When she did speak, Paige had to breathe deeply before she could gather up herself to answer the child.

"My daddy wanted to kill us. He said we weren't worth spit." Paige told her she was sorry for that, but she'd never do that. "I don't wanna die, Aunt Paige. If you think you'd like to kill me, could you just sell me off like Daddy wanted to do with us?"

Putting Emma on the couch next to her, she pulled the little girl into her arms. They both sobbed out their hurt at what Butch had done to his little family. When Heath came to get the baby, she and Mary held onto each other for a long time. It wasn't until Harris joined them that she realized Mary had cried herself to sleep.

Chapter 4

Conley was just pulling up his list of computers that he could hack into when Patty walked into his office. Well, he supposed walked wasn't the correct term. He simply appeared. The big faerie looked about as pissed off as he'd ever seen him, too. Smiling at the man as he put away his list, he asked him, politely, he thought, what the fuck he wanted.

"My mate." Conley asked him whatever he was talking about. "My mate. You have her, and I want her returned to me. I have done all I was required to do, and now our relationship is quit. Return her to me posthaste."

"Posthaste? My goodness, you do slip back into your time period when you're pissed off, don't you?" Tisking at the man, he picked up the notes he'd been working with earlier in the day before Patty had shown up. "The trouble is, I'm finding that the job you did for me isn't quite finished. You see, I'm no more in a position to take over the world than I was before. While I'm well aware that it wasn't your fault someone came and messed it up, you're still supposed to get me into that position so I can rule. I don't see that happening right now. Do you?"

Magic tightened around the room, but Conley didn't let it show that it bothered him. The hold that he had on this powerful being was slight at best. If Patty ever found out how slight it was, Conley knew he'd be dead before the creature's next heartbeat. He wasn't even sure why Patty hadn't figured out that going to any one of the people that had taken out the president would have helped him. Conley was happy he'd not and feared hourly that he would soon enough.

"Now that you've shown off your power let me tell you what it is I wish for you to do. I know. I know. That sounds like a favor. But it's not. You are going to do it, or your mate dies. Do I make myself clear? You've fucked me over quite enough, Patty, and I want results." No answer. However, like before, he tried very hard not to show how much it bothered him. "There is a man I want you to find. His wife is dead—she wouldn't play ball with me, and you can see where that got her. But this man, his name is James Avery. I want him dead. I don't care how you do it, but he must suffer, and badly. You'll go and see a woman by the name of Harrison Marshall. She's heading up the FBI right now, and as much as it pains me to say it, she's doing a good job. You tell her something like you're old friends with Avery, and she'll find him for you. She's a sap about shit when it comes to family and long friendships. Also, you'll record Avery's death so that I may be certain you're doing what I say. I will not take any excuses from you this time about not having any way to record the death. Figure it out."

Handing over a picture of the man, he waited on Patty to take it. Snatching it from his hand, Patty looked at it for a moment before putting it into his shirt pocket. When he only stood there, like he was waiting to be released or something, Conley lowered his head and pretended to work. It was the most fun he'd had with the man in all the time he'd worked for him.

Patty's wife, Mildred, had been easy enough to capture and take into his home. It had been purely by accident that he'd shot her when she'd been flying around in the woods where he hunted. At first, he thought he'd killed a large bat or something. But when he found her lying in the field, he wasn't sure even then what he had until she told him.

Conley didn't know how she had called out to

her mate, or even if she had. Honestly, he didn't really care, so long as they both understood that they were his until he said differently. And so long as he was getting what he wanted from them, he'd keep them guessing as to when he was going to allow them to be freed. Which, if he was honest with himself, was never going to happen. They were, as a pair, very valuable to him. Especially Patty.

Colonel Lakeside had been in the CIA for a couple of decades when he retired. There were other branches of service that he'd had a hand in helping out as well, he supposed. The man certainly had some great contacts. Man and woman, both retired and still serving that he seemed to be able to tap at any time when he needed some information. It was strange to Conley that no one had figured out why he had simply not run for office again but were, as a whole, very disappointed in the fact that he'd not.

Conley had had nothing to do with Patty's retirement from the services. It was just that he'd decided he would no longer work. However, Conley had a great deal to do with the reason Patty was still poking around the offices gathering information that seemed as personal and dangerous as anything he'd done *while* working. The CIA and FBI directors were other positions that Conley was going to eliminate as soon as he was in office. A great many others too, as a matter of fact. Why have those services around when he was going to be in charge of everyone? All things were going to fall into place when he became the dictator for life in the US.

As soon as he was able to kill off a few more of the operatives he had working for him, that was. They were tedious assholes and got in and out of places he didn't want them. Like the arrest of the men he'd had captured just before Conley had tried to kill Avery.

Avery had gone in without his permission and had gotten the men out. Just like he knew they were there for no crime. Not that he could have given him permission or even killed him for doing it. Avery was a hero. Everyone but him loved a hero.

It had nothing to do with the reasons he'd made up for them to be in the clutches of the monster overseas who just happened to be one of his contacts. It was his way of trading information they had, and he had wanted. Nothing wrong with a little free enterprising, right? At least not to him. With his plan to kill off all the undercover operatives that worked for the US, he'd be in power in no time at all. Who, he thought, was going to stop him? Well, there might be one or two that would try. However, Conley was saving Harrison Parker Marshall for last. He needed her, for the time being, at least.

She was, without her knowledge, the one

helping him the most. Or she had. Having the vice president arrested was a stroke of brilliance. Then figuring out that the president had his own agenda had made an opening for him to step right into the shoes of the man himself. However, the people were so outraged by the shenanigans that had gone on in the White House that they demanded accountability and a new vote. He'd been president for less than a month when he was outvoted, and a new, younger man was put in position. Christ, he hated Harrison as much as he needed her.

Getting to work, Conley thought about the things he'd done, how much he'd given up to be where he was today. Then, once he'd been in the position of a lifetime, he'd realized there was a great deal more out there than just this one job. That was when he set to work on getting things lined up in a nice, neat row to assure he was taken care of for the rest of his days. Not to mention the amount of work it had taken him to get the neat row set up.

Taking precautions and making hard sacrifices were the only reasons he'd not been caught. Not moving up in the modern age had kept him out of the view of people like Harrison and the others.

Conley typed on a manual typewriter he'd own since childhood. Everything he needed to send out from himself when he was at work was typed up on a single sheet of paper without carbon paper, one copy, and hung on the office bulletin board for everyone to read. Then someone, usually someone that didn't want to go around telling people of his memo or letter, would type it up on their own computer and send it out. Fine by him. He had no secretary to speak of and wouldn't want one even if there was one out there that was assigned to him to work. Memos, letters, and things were printed off for him, if he needed to be aware of something, by one of the other staff that worked in his area and laid on his desk.

He didn't use an electric typewriter, nor the computer he kept locked in the safe when there were others in and out of his office. No, there were ways to get whatever had been typed out on them traced back to him. Since he'd bought and paid for the laptop he used for espionage, he didn't figure anyone would need to know about it. And he was happy to admit to himself that it was espionage. It was his fun time, he thought to himself.

Then when he was finished with the ink roll on his old typewriter, he would burn the ribbon until there was nothing but a couple of pieces of metal. There were no carbon copies of things, no fax numbers for him to use. He supposed he had one of those, but that would get him caught, and he wasn't going to be caught.

There was no cellphone that he used or owned either. Not even a burner. He'd had a house phone for a while but had decided it was too much work to get up each time it rang. So that had gone out the door with the computer, tablet, and any other tracking device given to him when he'd taken over the job as speaker of the house. Conley once had a pager he'd had since he was a working man in the big city of Washington, DC. But like some of the other things he'd had, it had grown obsolete.

That was why he'd worked hard at cloning every computer in the big building. Getting to them with the laptop he hid in the safe in his office had been tedious but worth it. If he had something that needed to be sent out that would stir up some trouble, he'd simply log onto one of the other computers from his and send it from that person. With the exception of five. And those five pissed him off every time he thought about them.

He'd been to the Marshall home several times since the new administration had taken over. Each time he'd tried to get to Harrison's computer, someone would be in her large office for some reason. Even that big lummox of a husband of hers had a security lock on his that was giving him fits about getting unlocked too.

Then there was the president, vice president,

as well as the first lady, whose computers he hadn't gotten to. Christ, it was like they didn't trust him. Not that he thought they should, but they should have because of how he was their right hand man. Or so he let them believe.

He'd get them soon. He knew it. Even if he had to break into their offices and get to them. They were holding him up, and while he was going to be ruler, he wanted to do it before he was too old to enjoy it.

Just as he was putting his computer away, his office phone rang. Ignoring it to leave for the day, he thought about all the things he was going to do when he got home. After thinking about the memo he was going to send out to stir up trouble again, he decided he needed to work on it a bit more.

There wasn't any need for him to worry that Patty would do his job. Having his mate locked up in a stone room was going to keep him in line. Her too. Having her in the stone like room that he'd located near his home, Conley knew they couldn't communicate with each other. Thus her not being able to tell Patty where she was and having him come and get her. Christ, this was fun. Reminding himself to get some juice on the way home for the faerie, he smiled as he left the building and headed to his home. There he could plot and plan as he wanted.

~*~

Paige was just getting out of her car when she saw someone standing on her front porch. Not entirely sure if she was afraid or just annoyed, she called for Rebel, and whoever else was close to her to come to the house. Just as she was pulling the things from the back seat of the car, the man came to assist her.

"I've an issue I'd like to speak to you about." She asked him who he was. "You know me as Patrick Lakeside, I believe. It's as good a name as any that I've adopted over the years. I need to speak to you, but we can wait on the others that you've called in to tell them as well."

"You're a faerie. But not just a faerie, are you? Something stronger." He nodded as he took the bag she had away from her. "You can't hurt me. I want to make that clear right up front. I'm powerful in my own right, and the rest of this shadow is a great deal stronger than anyone knows of."

"I know. And I won't harm any of you, my lady. I believe you to be too valuable." They were in the house when Rebel appeared. The rest of them came to the house, couples at a time. When they were all seated in the living room, drinks and cookies there for them to eat, Patrick started talking to them. "I— Let me gather my thoughts for a moment." Tears of diamonds raced down his cheeks as he seemed to gather up an inner strength that was taking him under with it. "My mate has been murdered. She passed away just today, not an hour ago. I can no longer feel her heart beating as mine does. My heart is heavy, and I shall join her soon. But I wish to give you some information that will help you with a growing problem that has haunted me for several months. Conley Parker."

"The speaker of the house." He nodded at Shep. "I'm assuming you've been at his beck and call for all those months. While he—he killed her."

"Yes. He isn't aware that she has died as yet. You see, he's had her locked in a stone crypt. I couldn't go to her, nor her to me. But I could speak to her through our link. He, of course, didn't know this, but it did keep me from killing Parker for how he was treating the love of my life. Parker, he murdered her by taking the one thing from her that all faeries need. The sunlight that keeps our magic alive. His neglect murdered her as surely as if he'd pulled out a gun and shot her."

"I'm so very sorry." He thanked them all as they told him how sorry they were for his loss. Then Paige thought of something. "I'm assuming you're here to help us take him down. Why haven't you killed him yourself? I'm sure there will be no repercussions for killing him."

"No, there would not be. However, he must, as all humans should, pay for his crimes. Even if it's death by one of you." Patrick lost control again, and she got up to sit next to him. Before she could think of the consequences of her actions, she pulled him to her shoulder and hugged him. The blast of magic hit her hard, and she found herself hanging onto him rather than giving him comfort. "You aren't hurt, are you?"

"No. I don't know what that was, but I'm assuming it was from you." He smiled and nodded. When she looked around the room, wondering why no one was upset that she'd been blasted, it seemed that they'd all gotten whatever she had from the man. "You shared this, whatever it was."

"You shared. I only gave you the part of me that is magical. My goodness, you *are* powerful. More so now. I am glad I was able to give you this. You will use it wisely, I believe." Paige told him she'd do her best. "Thank you. While you are recovering from the magic, you will also find that you have all the information you need on Parker. Also that he is looking to find your brother. I had no idea that you were his sister until I was looking for Harrison. Another person that Parker wishes to be dead sooner rather than later."

"Why does he want James?" She looked at her brother as he leaned back on the couch with his eyes closed. Then it hit her. "He went to the pub to kill him because of some job he was on."

"The Americans that he and you, I'm assuming, liberated from the prison they were in. Parker traded them for someone he could control. Information as well. When they were released and brought back here, he had no more power over the country he sold them to. And by power, I mean guns and other munitions items." Paige got up to pace. She was thinking hard when James asked her if she had a plan. "I wish to contribute a part of the plan if you would. Also, I would very much like to be able to retrieve my mate's body so we can be taken to the faerie garden that has been made for the two of us."

"Tell us your plan." Harris smiled at Patrick when she added please to her demand. They took notes on the things he could help them with. "He wants to be dictator for life. Is that even possible?"

"You would know more than I would, I believe. Even if you cannot, there will be a great many people killed to get him in a position to test his theory. I wish for no one else to be harmed by this monster." Paige said she didn't either. "I don't believe he is even aware of you, Lady Paige. Or, for that matter, that this shadow is as powerful as it is now." Paige told him she was glad for that, at least. "You will take him down, will you not?"

"I'm thinking he needs to be dead more than paying for his crimes right now. But that's just me."

Everyone laughed, but it was a nervous laugh. "All right. We need to think and plan. I have what he's been up to, but I need more."

"I can get your wife out for you." Paige turned to Rebel when she spoke. "If you can tell me approximately where she is, I can get in and out without anyone knowing I was even there. Also, you'll need to tell me where to bring her when I have her."

"If you could bring her to the yard, the faeries can take her to the garden." Patrick got down on his knees and thanked Rebel for what she was doing for him. "I cannot thank you enough for what you have done for me. After I leave here, I will announce to the others my plan, and I shall join her."

Paige and the others went into the yard. Rebel left, in her usual way of popping out. There were several tense moments when she didn't return right away, and Paige was afraid she'd met up with Parker. But when she returned, the beautiful woman in her arms, Paige had a moment of clarity that she'd never had before. They were the king and queen of all faeries. And not only that, but the magic they'd been given, she'd bet they'd have help from all the elements should they need it.

"I've helped her a bit. You might have thought her dead, Patrick, but she was only shutting down."

Patrick went to his mate and held her in his arms as he sobbed. When a swarm of something came toward her, Paige only just stopped herself from swatting at them when she realized they were smaller versions of the couple on the lawn. "They'll help the two of you if you allow it, sir. I don't know a great deal about the little people, but I'm assuming they can do more for her than even I could when I picked her up."

The swarm, or pip, as Patrick said they were called, covered their queen from head to toe with their bodies. Their wings were moving so quickly while they helped her that it was like her skin was covered in wings, and she was alive with them. As soon as the queen drew in a deep startling breath, the little people scattered, but not too far. They would give all they were to keep the woman alive.

They all headed into the house again as the two of them sat on the ground, holding and kissing each other. She was weak, but she was also very glad to see her mate. Bella made sure there was plenty of juice for the queen and sugar for the faeries. As they entered the house again, Heath stopped Paige from joining the others in the kitchen to get snacks.

"Will you go after him?" She nodded. "Good. I don't want you to go, not really. But I do think you'd be the only one that could get in and out without anyone hurting you. Harris could, I suppose, but with her having a baby, I'd worry to death that she might hurt the baby."

"I agree. While you could have been a little more romantic about me going, I love you to pieces for just saying what you were thinking." He pulled her into his arms and kissed her. It was long, sexy, and full of heat. When he lifted his head, only to rest it on hers, she thought of all the things she wanted to do to this man. "I do love you, Heath. More than I thought possible. But if we don't find an hour for us to make love, I'm going to rape you right here in this room while your family is around."

He took her hand into his and dragged her to the kitchen. Heath kissed her on the mouth quickly, then looked at his family again. She'd never seen him so gung-ho before. Or rude.

"Harris, you and Shep can watch the kids tonight, right?" She nodded before Heath looked at the others. "Help her pack the kids up and then get out of here. I have a mate to make love to, and I think you all can understand that this is long overdue."

They were all laughing as they packed up the kids. Mary was a little tense to go with them, but when she was told about the cookie baking going on all day tomorrow, her and Angel gathered up the things they'd need and went with them. Grandda kissed her on the cheek as he walked by her, laughing the entire time.

When the doors were locked up, Heath picked her up in his arms and took her to the bedroom. For all his seeming need to hurry things up, he stood her on the floor gently and kissed her as just as gently. Then he got down on one knee in front of her.

"I love you so much, Paige, and I have waited what seems like forever to have you come into my life. And now that you're here with me, I can't imagine a life without you in it. Will you do me the honor not just being my wife, but being my partner, my lover, my friend, and the mother to our children?" She nodded, telling him she'd do all those things with him. "I'm not finished yet. Don't rush me, please."

"Yes, all right. But I'm needing you. If you take much longer, I'm going to find another way to make you mine." He grinned at her before kissing her hand. "I mean it, Heath. You're taking much too long."

"Such a romantic. I love you, Paige, and I wouldn't change a thing about you. Not ever." He pulled a blue bag out from under the bed. Getting down on her knees, she watched as he opened the bag and pulled out a smallish box. "I know you're a cat too, so I got you something that will not cut your finger off if you don't have a chance to take this off first. It has a chip in it too, so you can find it if it becomes lost."

He slipped it onto her finger, and the fit was

perfect. She loved it. Loved how it sparkled around the room from the overhead lights. The way the azure blue color seemed to be the exact hue of her eyes. The star, a blemish, it was called, was a perfect star and shone brightly against the stone's blue. There were diamonds on either side of the setting that set off the ring in the most perfect way possible.

"Look at the inside of the ring band." She did, pulling it off to see what he'd put inside. He said the words with her as she read the love he'd declared for her put in the language of their kind. "You are my air, my water, my blood. I love you, Paige Marshall."

When he stood up, pulling her upright as he went, Heath kissed her again. Gently, of course, but with such need that she could taste it. Lifting his head from hers, he picked her up by her ass and pressed her against the wall. All sense of taking it slowly went out the window when she felt his cock, hard and thick, at her pussy.

The sound of clothing tearing had her coming. She could feel his bare skin against her own as she ripped his shirt off, using a little of her beast to help. Their shoes were tossed away, their clothing in shreds all over the room. When Heath slammed into her, filling her to her throat, it seemed Paige let go of the primal scream that came from her very soul when she came.

Heath bit her breasts, her shoulders, and neck. Each place he nipped at her, Paige would come again. Even as he fucked her this way, she knew there was more. That when she hit her peak, one that she'd yet to feel, it would turn her inside out and back again. Throwing back her head when he buried his face at her pulse, Paige held him to her, hoping he'd take a bite out of her neck that would mark her for all time.

"I need you." She didn't know how to answer him, even if she understood if it was a question or not. "Now, I need to feel you riding me."

There was no kind of movement that she could feel. Finding herself on the bed, her body atop of Heath's, she had to breathe for a moment with this new position. He was deeper than before. His cock filled her out so that she felt stretched to the limit. As soon as he sat up, pulling her hips up, she began to ride him faster and faster until she thought she'd come a hundred times before he flipped her to her back.

"Come for me." She screamed again, her throat raw for each time she'd come. "Come again for me, Paige, and I'll join you, so we're one."

Her body seemed to not just have a mind of its own but know what to do to join Heath. Bowing up, her back ramrod stiff, she held onto Heath as her nails, the claws of her cat, dug deeply into his arms, drawing blood. When he threw back his own head, his claws held her still while she felt him coming, his body emptying into hers so hotly that Paige just blinked out.

Waking up, she was glad to know she'd only been out for a few seconds. Heath was atop her still, his breathing hard and labored. When he rolled to his back, taking her with him, she landed on his chest. Hearing his heart pounding as hard as hers was, Paige thought that if she were to be asked about any other sex she'd had before today, she'd tell them it was as unrememberable as this one was memorable. Christ, she had never come so hard in her life.

"If we do this all the time, I'm going to be looking like an old man before my time." She didn't even have the strength to raise her head and look at him when he spoke. "If I had known it was going to be like this, I might well have taken you a good deal sooner. I swear to you, Paige, I'm dead."

She giggled. Raising up her head, about all she could manage, she looked at her mate. "The mattress is ruined. There are claw marks on the head and footboard. Blood all over both of us, and I find that I don't care one bit. Not even for the teasing that is going to ensue when we meet up with your family again." She laughed again. "That is if we can ever have enough energy to move anytime soon."

Paige thought for sure as she fell back to sleep that the two of them would do this all the time. Taking sex to the next level. She found she didn't care, either. It was so relaxing to be as sated as she was right now.

Chapter 5

Heath didn't want to admit that he was sore. In fact, every time he moved around and pulled another place in his body that ached, he had to smile. Christ, they'd been animals last night. Pulling the bassinet toward him to put Emma back and take George from it, he looked over at Angel and Mary. They were looking at a magazine that had come in the mail today.

"Have you found anything in there that you want Santa to bring you for Christmas?" Mary told him not to be daft. There wasn't a Santa Claus. "Who told you that? Of course, there is one. He is right now figuring out what you want for Christmas. You can help him along by marking the things you see there in that toy magazine."

Angel rolled her eyes, not even hiding the fact that she thought he was nuts. It was all he could manage not to burst out laughing at her. When

George was finished with his bottle and burped, he laid him in the little crib with his sister. The two of them immediately reached for each other.

Standing up to stretch, he saw that the older girls were still thumbing through the catalog, so he left them to it to see about lunch. Paige had left an hour ago to meet up with Harris and James. He was ready to get going on a couple of things he had in the works too. Grandda showed up just as he was putting corndogs on a plate for Mary and her sister.

"What on earth is that thing?" He told his grandda what the kids were eating. "You're kidding me. A hotdog wrapped up in cornbread. Sounds like a good waste of cornmeal if you ask me." Of course, the girls were delighted with their great grandda.

"Would you like one?" Of course, the face he made had all three of them laughing hard enough to make Heath remember his sore body. Asking what Grandda wanted gave his ribs a chance to rest and him to sit again. "When are you leaving for the cruise? I wish I could go with you, Grandda. You guys are going to have a blast."

"I surely hope so. I'm really looking forward to it. The reason I'm here is to ask you if you'd mind having a look in on the Older Than Dirt Club for me." Heath asked him if that was the name he'd come up with for his workers. "Not me, but them guys did it. They said if they were going to be in a club, they wanted people to stay out of their business who wasn't old like them. I'm older than all of them, and I surely think anyone looking at me would be able to see that."

They both laughed as he got up to make Mary a second corn dog. "I don't mind helping you out with that. So long as they understand, I'm not joining but making sure they have work to do." He handed him a list. "What's this, Grandda?"

"Jobs that the people around want to have finished up. I was thinking that next spring, I'd hire a few teenagers to help tote and haul off wood and things for people. There is a lot of fallen stuff from a while back that needs a pickup. Also, I was thinking we'd sell the bigger pieces of wood for the kids for their own use. Everyone, I think, could use some pocket money from time to time." Heath agreed with him. "There is talk about town that someone bought the old grade school. I hadn't realized we'd gotten that far yet."

"I think Harris bought it when it came up at the meeting a couple of weeks ago. The other building we're going to put up is well on its way to being started. The way they're working, I'm thinking it'll have the outside walls all in before January." Grandda took a slice of bread from the cabinet and pulled out some jelly he'd picked up when they'd cleaned out Mom's house. "Who had you heard that from? I mean, anyone just speculating, or someone causing trouble?"

"Trouble, I'd imagine. But I nipped that in the bud right away. That job I got working at the grocery surely does put me in the thick of things." Heath agreed with him. "We're leaving in the morning. Flying down to the port then going out that afternoon. Never been on a cruise before, nor have the kids. I'm surprised they're allowed to go with me, to be honest."

"I was as well." Grandda ate his jelly sandwich as the girls went to the living room again. "They don't believe in Santa. I was seeing if they'd mark up the catalog we got in the mail yesterday. I think this might be harder than having them believe in him."

"I've been thinking on that. You should have a letter from the man in red, so they'll see that he writes to kids. Your momma used to do that. She'd send it out a couple of weeks before Thanksgiving to warn you guys that he was keeping an eye on you. I'd not say that to them—might well scare them a bit." Heath said he could see that with his girls. "Might also be that no one has taken the time much in making sure they had themselves a nice Christmas. I can see their momma trying her best. That daddy of theirs, he should have been shot a long time ago. But then

I'd not have me four little grandbabies around to play with."

"I love them all so much, Grandda, that it hurts me when I think of the way Dad treated us when we were younger." Grandda nodded but did put out his handkerchief to blow his nose. "You all right? You're not missing him, are you?"

They'd all decided that their dad wasn't going to be mentioned by name, and they'd stuck to it. But right now, Heath was worried that not having their dad around was taking its toll on Grandda. When he got up and poured himself some tea, Heath waited. Grandda would get to it sooner or later. He just needed to wait for him to get his words all straight in his head.

"I think about him at times, like when I'm holding onto one of the babies. Having a conversation like you and me are having now. I don't miss him, not really, but I do think about what he's missing. How he's not ever going to see them kids that are calling me Grandda." Grandda sipped his tea. "I don't want him around none, as you can guess. He'd be putting his nose up with those children in the other room like he found them to be inferior or something. Stupid jackass. When all along, them kids, all of the kids, are a durn sight better than he'd ever have been had he been around. He was a putz, Heath. I can say that now. It wasn't just my lovely Jill Ann that he hurt, but everyone he came in contact with. I hear some of the crap he did to others while I'm working, and I'm ashamed that he was my son."

"I'm sorry about that, Grandda." He knew he'd wave him off and wasn't disappointed when he did it. Just as he was getting up to hug his grandda, Angel came into the room with them.

"Whatcha got there, honey?" She showed Grandda what she'd been looking at while Heath got her a glass of juice to drink. "Well, now. That's a right pretty bedroom set you picked out there. Reminds me of the woods around here. All warm and cozy. Is this something you'd like to have in your own room? I'm sure that your...what do you call my grandson and Paige?"

"Uncle and aunt. I don't want it for my room. I like white, but Mary loves it. She said it reminds her of the trees we'd hide in when Daddy was rampaging. Momma called it that when he was upset with something. Which, if you asked me, was just about all the time." Angel got up on Grandda's lap when he offered it to her. "We never had a Christmas tree before, Grandda Sheppard. Do you suppose if we're good, one will come here?"

"That's not the way it works, honey. Who told you that part?" Neither of them had to be told it was

Butch that had lied to the kids, so neither he nor his grandda were surprised when Angel told them. "You and your aunt and uncle will be going out in the woods and picking out a right pretty tree to use. Then you'll decorate it all up with balls and stuff and make it so pretty it'll hurt your eyes when the lights are on."

Mary joined them in the kitchen then, taking Grandpa's other knee as he explained about how the tree was decorated and the fun they'd have doing it. When asked if he'd help, Grandda had to turn away for a moment before he was able to tell them he would be there with bells on. He also told them he had some ornaments that Heath had made when he was a little guy.

Heath was enjoying the conversation between the three of them when Paige spoke to him. She sounded happy, so he didn't freak out when she asked him how close he was to the computer in her office.

I'm here with Grandda. What do you need? He told Grandda where he was headed as he told Paige what he was doing here. *I really want to run out and get a tree now for them so they can see one. It sucks that they didn't get anything either, not even a tree. It should have been in the house no matter what. I do wish I'd known about your sister before she died. Perhaps we could have saved her.*

I try not to think about that. It hurts my soul when I think about how much she needed me, and I was out of the country. Did I tell you today that I love you? Heath said she had, and he was glad to hear it again. And that he loved her. *You're the best of the best. All right. Let me tell you what I need for you to look up for me.*

They spent the better part of an hour going over the things she'd stored on a thumb drive that had been hidden from prying eyes. It had been in one of the many pickups that Rebel had helped her with. On it were her contacts, as well as any orders that had been sent to her. She'd take a picture of them, then send it to the thumb drive when she was at a place that was secure. Right now, he was looking for connections from Parker to the vice president, if there had been any.

So he knows him but is not connected with him. I couldn't remember what I thought about when I wrote notes. Only that I had them. He asked her what she wanted him to do now. *Nothing you can do, really. We're going over the information I was given from Patrick and seeing where the dots connect. So far, there are no dots connecting him to anyone inside the White House. He has some oddball things he does where he thinks it's keeping him hidden away from getting caught. Also, and this was what I think is so fucking funny, he thinks that no one knows about the computer he has hidden away in his office. Moron.*

When he was finished doing what she needed, they closed the connection, and he went to find his kids. There wasn't anyone in the kitchen, so heading to the living room, he heard his grandda speaking. He'd bet it was mostly to himself. Heath paused to listen to what he was saying.

"Now, now, little man. There is no reason for you to start that stuff up. Them sisters of yours are napping, and you're making a fuss." He heard the chair creak and then George making a fussing noise. "You lay that head of yours here on Grandda, and we'll both take us a nap too. I don't blame you one iota for not wanting to be all wrapped up with your sister. A man needs room, now, don't he?"

Heath found himself smiling and crying at the same time. Grandda playing with the kids was something he did all the time. But hearing him talk to one of them when no one was around hit home to him that his grandda didn't care one bit that they weren't his biological great-grandchildren. They were his, and Grandda wouldn't treat them any differently than he would Shep's baby when it came around. It felt good to know that.

The five of them were asleep when he snuck in and took pictures of them. The girls were on the floor at Grandda's feet, while the babies, both of them, were snuggled up under his chin. It was moments like this when he missed his mom the most. She'd be all over those kids and not have one bit of regret in spoiling them rotten either.

When Paige returned home, she looked exhausted. They were going to have tacos for dinner tonight, and he was looking forward to it. It was one of those really messy meals that he enjoyed once in a while. Besides, the girls had never had them. He realized he'd forgotten to go to the jailhouse to talk to Butch for Alan—he was going to be the attorney for the kids. Doing it before dinner seemed the best bet. Heath decided to walk there and enjoy one of the nice evenings before it got too cold for walks.

Heath was told that Butch was in a mood, whatever that meant, for it didn't have any bearing on what he needed to ask him. Alan had given him a list this morning and wanted to see if Heath could get him some answers. The fact that he and Belinda were never married in the first place made things both easier and harder for the old vampire. Heath was glad to be able to help.

"You told the police you were married to Belinda, is that right?" Butch asked him how that was his business. "Because I said it is. Were you married to her or not? Not only can we not find a marriage license that has been filed, but your name is not on either of Belinda's oldest children's birth certificates. Why is that?"

"She'd get all fired up, and I'd hit her around

about it, then she'd just go and do as she damned well pleased anyway. Then she'd just file away them licenses, and it'd be too late for me to be put there as their daddy. How is it my fault that I had to knock her around a little?" Heath told him it was his fault, and he should have been arrested a long time ago. "Well, she knew better than to do that to me. You or them police, they put my name on my boy's certificate, didn't they? I told them to. But police always want to do the opposite of what is right. You know if someone is trying to get me out of here?"

"Only to get you to a larger prison, that's all. Just so you're aware, you're not named on the certificates of any of Belinda's children. Not the newborns either. They're a girl and a boy, as you are aware of, so about your thoughts of having the son come to you — even if that were remotely possible — you'd not be named as his father. I, for one, am glad about that. What about a marriage license? Is there one of those floating around?" Butch laughed and said he'd said there was plenty enough that it should be true. "So that's a no as well."

"It's not like I could have married her anyway. I done already had me a wife." Heath asked where she was. "I don't rightly know anymore. She lit out one day right after a particularly huge fight over me having a steak dinner and her wanting to spend the money better than on one meal for me. You know women, they'll buy all kinds of things to cook with, but they'll pitch a bitch when you ask them to cook you a steak. She'd been going on about how one steak could feed us for a week. Damned women. I don't even know why I try to live with them. They're nothing but pains in the ass if you ask me."

"I'm sure where you're going, that won't be an issue anymore. Anything else I should know about your married life? Is there another wife or two out there someplace." He said just one more. But she was dead. "Did you kill her?"

"Not my fault. She was bitching." He laughed. "I'm thinking I need to pick me a better kind of woman. One that can't talk. That way, I might be able to get through a day without knocking one around. Maybe."

After leaving Butch, Heath gave all the information to Alan, including the names of his other two wives. Then when he got home, he needed to not just shower but to scrub his skin until it hurt. Being around that man made him feel all kinds of nasty.

~*~

Shannon was ready to go back to Ohio. The house, thanks greatly to her best friend Lily, was sold almost the same day it was put on the market. Donating her mother's clothing and most of her own, she didn't have but a few things to pack up to take back with her. Hoping she'd have a nice place to stay right away, Shannon looked around the place one more time and thought about the memories that she and her mom had made in this place.

When she'd been born, her mother hadn't been much more than a child herself. But as she'd been kicked out of her parents' home, her mom had done all she could, on her own, to keep the two of them fed and with a roof over their heads. Then, when Shannon started to make money, they'd purchased the house and had continued their lives together. This trip, the one to Florida to take a cruise, had been a birthday gift and Christmas gift combined for her and her mom.

Locking the door and putting the key in the lockbox hanging there, Shannon made her way to her rental car. Driving back to Ohio would take her a couple of days longer, but taking her art supplies on the plane and hoping they'd not get broken was too much of a chance. Besides, she told herself, she'd get to see the countryside in all its colors. She might even take a few pictures while she was at it.

Stopping for lunch seemed like a good idea, so she pulled into the diner once more before leaving town for good. She and her mom had eaten there at least once a week since she could remember. They also had the best warmed cider. Just as she gave her order to Penny, the only waitress on duty, Reed Herbert sat down across from her.

Reed had been working for her since she started going on a circuit. She'd gone out with him when it was necessary for her to be at a gathering, but for the most part, she didn't have a great deal to do with the man. Not that he wasn't good at his job, but sometimes she had a feeling he forgot who paid him.

Just as her salad was brought to her, he took it from her. "A woman like you needs to eat better, Shannon, honey. I was just thinking the other day that you need to be putting on a little more weight. Now that I see you here, I can tell you need to put on a great deal. You're much too thin." She took her salad back and told him she was just fine. "We'll let it slide this time. I was wondering something else. I think for all I do for you, I should be getting a cut of what you sell at these galleries you're in now. It's mostly due to the fact that I've put your name out there. It's only reasonable that I get a cut too. I was thinking, since it's my work you're living off of, that it should be fifty-fifty."

"No." She ate her salad and pushed the bowl away. "It's my work that is paying your salary, Reed. Why are you even here today? I thought you had a job you worked when you're not working for me."

"I lost it a couple of weeks ago. For that, I'm

putting the blame on you too. I was taking a client out to lunch to get him to take you on, and I had one or two more drinks than I should have. But now that I've had time to think it over, I'm wondering why I've not gone full time with you anyway. As I said, it's a job that gives you time to eat lunch out and not be working." She didn't bother giving him an answer if there had even been a question. "What do you say to the partnership idea?"

Shannon had never seen this side of Reed before. Usually, he was polite and didn't speak about money. He did with her attorney when he needed something like gas money or a ticket to someplace, but never her. When she put her hand out to reach for her glass of pop, he put his hand over hers and dug his nails into the top of it.

"You're hurting me. Let me go this minute before you get your ass fired." He said she wasn't going to fire him. She needed him too much. Then he mentioned the partnership again. "No. We have a contract, Reed. You get paid a flat salary, and I— You're hurting me."

He'd drawn blood. Even as his nails dug deeper into her flesh, she could feel her wrist being bent at an odd angle that had her thinking he was going to break her wrist. Not having any idea what to do, she started to call out to Penny when he snapped one of her fingers.

"You'll keep that trap of yours shut." She nodded, tears flowing down her cheeks at the pain she was in. "Now, I'm going to ask you once again, and you're going to tell me that we're going to be partners. Then you and I are going to go over to the bank, and you're going to take out all the money and hand it over to me. Or I break your hand in a way that you never paint again." She asked him why he was doing this. "Because, my dear artist, I'm broke. I had the best of both worlds and lots of money coming in until you fucked me over."

"How did I fuck you over?" He told her, tossing a napkin over her hand when Penny brought her the lunch she'd ordered. Tightening his grip on her wrist, she told Penny everything was all right. "You can't be serious. How do you think it's my fault that you lost your job because you returned to work drunk? I don't even know where your head is right now."

Spittle was falling out of his mouth as he spoke to her in a dangerous tone that made her terrified of him. Just as she was going to be sick, she felt something, a small touch to her mind, and waited.

Honey, it's Sheppard. You remember me telling you that we had a connection now, don't you? I can feel your terror. What is it you need for this old man to do for you? She told him that Reed was hurting her. Mostly she told Reed that he was hurting her, not really understanding how to talk to Sheppard. *You just think about what you want me to know, darling, and I'll get it. This Reed person, he in your house? Is he someone you know?*

Spilling everything that had happened since he joined her at the table, Shannon cried when she told him what he was planning to do with her money. Then she screamed, in her mind or out of it, she wasn't sure, when another finger was broken.

"Please. Help me, please." She was dizzy with the pain now and thought for sure she was seeing things when someone just appeared behind Reed. Whoever she was, she was speaking, but the words were making no sense to her pain-filled mind. Finally, unable to hold back any longer, Shannon threw up on the table. Then there was nothing.

Waking up, she screamed, sure that she was going to look at her hand and see it taken off at the elbow. Looking around, two cute little girls were staring at her and Mr. Sheppard. He was holding a baby in his arms that was drinking down a bottle like it was starved.

Sitting up all the way, she looked around. "What's happened? Where am I?" Sheppard told her that she was at the home of one of his grandsons. "Where is Reed? He was hurting me, and then a woman showed up. Where is he now? Jail, I hope?"

"Yes, jail. The woman was my granddaughter-in-law, Paige. She's Heath's wife. That's the house you're in. These are his children. Your hand? Well, that was fixed up too, so you'd not hurt." Looking at her hand, she didn't see any kind of wound, nor did she see where there was any kind of swelling. She asked Sheppard how she'd gotten here. "Well, now, that's a bit more involved. Rebel brought you here, as a matter of fact. And she was able to fix up your hand for you so you'd be able to use it. That monster there, he'd broken a few bones before Paige was able to arrive with Rebel."

"I don't know what made him do that. He's never been mean to me like he was there. Demanding things that I had no idea what he was doing." She glanced at the kids who were staring at her wide eyed. "He was breaking my hand and hurting me. I called to your grandda to help me, and he did."

"He's the best. We've been playing quietly while you rested. Except for Emma. She was doing her business in her diaper and making all kinds of noise." It took Shannon a moment to realize what the little girl was talking about. She burst out laughing when little Emma, the baby dressed all in pink, let loose some more gas. "I think she's been saving it up so her and Grandda could have a contest. They sure do stink up a room."

Delighted not to be hurting and with the children, she asked if she could have a drink of water. As she made her way to the kitchen, Mary, she was told her name was, came with her. Angel kept up a running sentence of what they'd been doing since she had arrived.

The kitchen was empty but for a single man. She backed away from him when he turned toward her so quickly.

"I won't harm you." Shannon took another step back when he took one towards her. "I swear to you on my mother's heart, I'd never harm you in any way. I think you might be my mate. I mean, you are my mate."

Too much, her mind screamed at her, and Shannon did something she'd never done before. Fainted dead away. Just as she was closing her eyes, the man grabbed her. Shannon was not having a good day.

Chapter 6

Trenton was just finishing up sweeping his office when someone knocked on his door. He knew that whoever it was didn't know him, or they would have walked right in. Most of his family was like that, being so familiar with their homes to be comfortable enough to walk in. Opening the door after looking at the person standing there, he leaned against the jam while he waited for the man to turn around. When he did, Trenton knew just who he was.

"Christ, I hope the other guy looks worse." He glared. "Buddy, unless you want your other eye black and the rest of your lip busted up, be nice. What are you doing here at seven in the morning on a weekday? I have things to get to."

"I do as well. I'm here looking for Shannon Hutchison. They told me at the jailhouse that she was staying in one of the big houses on this street." Trenton said he didn't know where she was. "Sure, you don't. She owes me for having me arrested, and then I need to find someone by the name of Paige. That's all I got from her when she hit me with her gun. She should be in prison. They have rules for carrying around a gun and hitting people with it."

"I know they do. And if anyone knows that rule, it would be Paige. She's not here either. And before you ask, no, I don't know where she is." The man said he was rude. "Perhaps I am, but I'm not the one looking for information and being a shit about it. Why don't you go back to the jailhouse and leave me to my work?"

As he started to close the door, the man put his foot in the door. Trenton, usually in a good mood, was glad that he was this particular morning. If it had been yesterday, he might well have torn the man's leg off at the hip. Opening the door just enough that he could see the grinning man, Trenton doubled up his fist and slammed it into the man's face.

Instead of closing the door and finishing up his chores, Trenton stepped out onto the porch and looked at the fallen man. His cursing, not nearly as fluent as any of the women in the family, had him laughing. Reaching for anyone close to him, he told them who he thought was at his door.

Well, he's no longer at the door but lying out on the

deck. Had the nerve to try and force his way into my house. He's looking for Shannon and Paige. I think he's stupider than I thought if he's planning on tangling with either of them right now. James said they were both with him and going over some things. *All right. I'm not sending this jerk there unless you wish to take him on. I know better than to try and protect one of the women in this house. They'd skin me alive if I tried.*

Trenton was sitting on the porch swing when Reed, he'd found out for sure his name was, sat up. His face was already swollen, but now he looked as if he might well have swallowed a couple of bees. When Reed stood up, he glared at him but didn't move to try to hurt him. Perhaps he could be taught.

"I suppose you think this is funny. To hit a man when he's down. I'm going to own your ass." Trenton only nodded as he heard the crunch of gravel under tires coming up his lane. "Where are they? I demand that you tell me right now, or I'm calling the police."

"That looks like them now. The police, not the women. I'd not fuck with them either if I were you. Paige is sort of touchy about things nowadays, and I don't know Shannon well enough to gauge her anger at you, but I'd lay low until I figured her out." Reed said he wasn't laying low, that they owed him. "Well, I do hope you have your will made out properly. Because as I said, you fuck with them, and you're going to be dead."

Officer Flagg got out of his car and took his time doing it. Reed was steaming by now. He was so pissed. Trenton didn't care so long as he didn't do anything more stupid. Filling out the paperwork when someone had to be killed was a pain in the ass. Rocking back and forth, he watched Reed make his way toward Ronny.

Ronny was a good old boy kind of cop. He was smart too. He kept up on all the newest laws, and he took refresher courses when they were offered. Trenton knew for a fact that Ronny even went to talk to the prisoners at the prison in order to keep his mind sharp when it came to thinking like a criminal. It must have worked because Ronny would be asked to come to the bigger cities to help solve a crime or two at least once a year.

"Whatcha doing there, Trent? Sure is a purty morning to be sitting out on the deck here. All we need is a couple of donuts and a good, nice pretty young thing to bring us out some tea to go with them." They both laughed as Reed kept going on about how he'd been hit twice and that he wanted to press charges. "He sure does go on about stuff, don't he? I nearly had me a mutiny on my hands when he didn't get himself a good lunch yesterday. He and them officers I got now might have been drawing guns at noon or something."

"He came here looking for Paige and Shannon. He told me that someone at the police station told him they were here." Ronny said he'd not gotten that from his place. "I know that. But I wanted to make sure you knew. Someone must have pointed him—"

"Are you two finished cutting the shit or whatever it's called? I want to talk to Shannon Hutchison. And I want to press charges against that piece of shit, Paige. She hit me with her pistol yesterday and had me arrested for no reason." Ronny stood up and stretched. Few people knew that Ronny was a bear—until they fucked with him anyway. "What the hell do they feed you guys around here? Steaks right off the fucking cow at birth? Where is Shannon? We'll start with her."

"She's decided to terminate your working relationship with her. Shannon seems like a nice girl, and you really got nasty with her." Reed rolled his eyes. "Also, Paige is Fed. So if she pulled a gun on you, then I'd say you must have needed it."

"Shannon can't terminate our contract. I have a good relationship with her, and I'll not allow her to...I don't want her to end things like we did. I was a little loud and rough, I can admit that, but there isn't any reason whatsoever for her to think this is a good reason to end my—her career over this." Ronny asked

Reed what it was that Shannon needed him for. "She's an artist. A very good one, too, I don't mind saying. I get paid a good amount of money, I'll say that, but I believe, and everyone I spoke to said, that I should be getting a percentage of her sales. I do just as much work as she does, and all she does is put a little paint to some canvas and makes out like a millionaire."

Trenton pulled out his phone and looked Shannon up. Normally he'd not sneak information on a family member unless it was necessary. As soon as he saw some of her work, he poked Ronny and showed him. Shan—all she was known by in the art world—was damned good. Trenton reached out to Paige and asked her how long she'd be.

Not long now. What did you need? He told her what was going on and what Reed was saying. *We can take a few minute break to come over there and work the man over. I think I got short changed when it came to beating the shit out of him. Your mate has a good right fist.*

She's not my mate. She's your brother's mate. Silence. It was so loud he was sure there was some sort of hole in the universe that had sucked all the sound out of it. *Are you there, Paige?*

My brother has a mate. Trenton didn't know what to say to that, so he said nothing. *He didn't say anything — well, neither did she, now that I think on it. We all just assumed she was your mate because of the way she smells. Are you sure she's James's — never mind. I know you're sure. We'll leave here now and be there in about ten minutes. We've gotten things worked out with Conley — James has a mate?*

Yes. And all right. But I'd not dally in getting here. Reed is acting all kinds of stupid right now, and I think he's going to be arrested again. He's fucking around with Ronny. And while he'll take it for a while, he won't allow him to curse at him much longer. She said they were leaving now. *Good. I'm sorry about you finding out about Shannon this way. I thought he'd tell you. Or at least she would.*

True to her word, they were there in no time. Even Grandda and Shep showed up around the time they did. Reed was dancing from Paige to Shannon, trying to get them to tell Ronny what had gone down at the restaurant yesterday. So far, all he was managing to do was piss even more people off. James came up on the deck from around the back of the house and sat down next to him on the swing.

"You didn't tell your sister." James said that Shannon had asked him to wait. "I see. Actually, I don't, but that's all right. Whatever she needs is fine with me."

"Thanks. By the way, I'll need a house if you know any around. I'll need to have a pretty good sized one with my kids still living at home." James watched

Reed talking at, not to, Shannon. "I haven't any idea if I should step in or keep my distance. Pissing off the women of your family can have brutal and painful consequences."

"You got that right. I'd wait for her to look at you. That is usually what I see happening when one of the others need something. Which isn't often, so keep watching her. But all bets are off if he touches her, right?" James just growled, the only warning he got that things had gone from talking to touching. "James, don't kill him with the police here."

James leapt from the swing, shifting to his cat and sending him flying. Trenton was just getting his feet under him when Reed was on the ground, and a large, very pissed off jaguar was sitting on his chest. Shannon was on the ground as well, but not from James. Thankfully. James would never have forgiven himself if he'd hurt his new mate. It was Billy who came to stand next to his dad when the translation was needed.

"My dad, the big cat on you, said that you're a piece of shit. I can say that on accounta my dad said I was to tell you word for word what he's saying. My goodness, mister, you sure are all kinds of dumb, aren't you? Anyway, he said you were warned not to touch her no less than three times. When you knocked her to her— Are you sure, Dad?" He must have gotten an answer. "All right, you knocked her to her ass. You went too far. Now you have to pay."

"Can you translate for me when your dad has something to say, Billy?" Trenton stood up when Shannon spoke. Whatever was going to happen, it would set the tone for hers and James's relationship. "James Avery, you're crushing this idiot. Not that I think the world wouldn't be a better place without his ass around, but to kill him here, in front of the police no less, isn't the way I'd like to start this relationship, or whatever the fuck this is. Let him go so the nice policeman—"

"You're his mate?" Harris and the others seemed as shocked as he was when James had told him. Harris especially. When she looked at Trenton, he shrugged. "I thought she was going to be your mate. I mean, that's the way it happens. Right?"

"I think it happens the way it happens. I need to talk to this fool, then we have some work to do." Shannon turned back to the two men on the ground. "Now, Reed, I'm going to tell you once more that you're fired. Where you got the idea that you deserved half of the money I make on a painting is beyond me. But that is not going to happen. Since you're in breach of contract for being a full blown ass, you're no longer entitled to any of the perks you were to get at the end of our relationship. I've called my attorney, and he will be notifying you soon. At the jail, I'm assuming, because I am pressing charges against you again."

"Dad asked—he said to make sure you knew he was asking you politely if you'd help him find a house for us all to live in together. My brother and sister are gone right now on a cruise. They're going to bust a gut when they get back and find out we got ourselves a pretty woman in the house." Billy looked at his dad, then looked back at Shannon. "I'm sorry. Dad said you're a lovely woman, and that I'm to behave myself or I'll be in Dutch with you."

"You're doing just fine, Billy. Thank you for helping me." James rolled off Reed, and Trenton laughed when Reed curled up in a tight ball. James must have gotten him in the nuts perfectly while getting up, and it was no less than the other man deserved. "As for the house, I'm not sure what is going to happen right now. I do need a place to be able to work. And it will need to be— I guess that can be discussed later. I'd like to press charges against Reed, Officer Flagg. I don't think there is a way to press charges because he's a dickhead, but I would like it so he can't come around me anymore. I don't need this sort of crap with everything else that is going on."

"Yes, ma'am, I can get that paperwork all sewn up for you. The judge will be the one that you ask to keep this here feller away from you. But I doubt you'll be bothered with him again anytime too soon." Ronny picked Reed up with one hand and shook him hard enough that his teeth rattled. Then he put him in the back of the cruiser while Reed was still bitching about poor treatment. "James, you bring your pretty lady down to the stationhouse so's she can fill out the paperwork on this mess here. It gets harder and harder to want to get out of bed in the morning when you know the kind of stuff you might encounter with folks. Yessiree bob, it sure is a mess with humans."

After Ronny left with Reed, James went to the side of the house, and Trenton handed him a bag of clothing. They didn't speak — Trenton knew the other man was embarrassed. But almost as soon as he was dressed, he asked if he could help him with the house.

"Just to find a few to look at for us to start with. She didn't say no to the idea — Trenton, I have a mate again. I didn't...I wasn't a cat when I married Sara. I thought I loved her, but not when we started out. She was pregnant with Beth, and the thing to do was to marry her." Trenton looked to the right when James did. "The house. I guess something close to here. And Paige. I need to be around my sister as much as I need to be able to breathe."

"I understand that. And I think there are three or four homes between here and my brothers' homes." He thanked him. "James, it's going to be all right. You'll see. She'll be a perfect match for you and your children."

"I think so as well."

As the other man made his way into the house, Trenton wondered what sort of baggage his own mate would bring to the table. It would be epic, or it would be nothing. Either way, he was starting to get excited about having her come around to be with him. It was lonely being the odd man out. Smiling, he thought it was also enlightening to be the only brother without a mate. Trenton was learning what he hoped was the correct way to woo and love a mate when she did come around.

~*~

Conley was making his way back to his office when he was stopped no less than four times to answer questions. While he was glad someone thought he'd know what the answer was, he didn't like to be bothered. He had a routine, and they were fucking it up talking to him all the time. Conley was going to add that to his list. No talking to him unless he spoke first. People should just keep their mouths shut all the time was his way of thinking. However, he'd never get a thing done if he were to impose that sort of rule all the time.

There were no people hanging around his office. Not that they ever did, but he was glad he had a straight shot to not just his office but quiet time. As he was unlocking the door, something that was frowned upon, he heard someone say his name. Turning, pissed off already, he was dismayed to find Mr. President standing right behind him.

"Hello, Parker. You're running behind, aren't you? Someone told me that someone could set their watch by you being on time. I have a few things I'd like to go over with you." He wanted to snarl at the man and demand who had spoken to him about his habits. He did correct the man that his name was Conley Parker, not Parker Conley. "I'm aware of your name. How about we head into your office now."

Unlocking the door, he nearly snapped his key off when it didn't open as easily as he thought it should have. Of all mornings to have this happen, today wasn't a good day. Moving into his office, he stopped right inside the doorway to look around. The bump from behind him had Conley going into the room and having the door closed behind him. He turned to look at Mr. President and found himself looking into the face of Patty.

"What have you done? Look at this mess. You're going to clean this up, or so help me I'm going to murder that wife of yours." He didn't like the grin on his face. Nor the knowing look he had when he looked around. "You're not going to get away with this. I hope you're aware of that."

"What I'm aware of is that you no longer have my mate. And that while she's weak, Mildred is doing much better. You could have killed her the way you had her locked up like you did. No sun was bad enough, but you didn't allow her to have any juice or fresh fruit." Conley said he'd picked some up for her but simply didn't get around to giving it to her. "I told you that when you took her that she needed sunlight and fresh juice. If not for the help of some very powerful people, she would have died." Conley thought she was dead. When he'd remembered to check on her a couple of days after buying the juice for her, she was gone. In her place was a bunch of flowers. "Sit there in that chair that has been readied for you."

"Let's talk this over, Patty. I mean, she's not dead. That's good. But there isn't any reason for us to be enemies. Everyone takes terrible steps to get ahead." Patty told him once again to sit. "I don't want to sit there and hear you lecture me on what I should and shouldn't have done. Now, you go on home to that mate of yours and—"

"Sit the fuck down." He did. Right on the chair that hadn't been behind him when he was stalling. "Now. I'm going to do two things for the people that helped me with my mate. Then Mildred is going to come here and take what she thinks is worth you having her locked up. It's only fair, don't you think, that she gets her part of you?"

"Is she going to kill me?" Patty simply told him yes. Nothing more, just that single word. "I'm a very important man. She won't be able to get away with that. I have friends in high places that are going to miss me."

"No, they won't. No one will."

The woman who had come into view from behind Patty didn't strike fear in his heart. In fact, his cock got just a little hard when he saw her in the form fitting flat black body suit.

Every curve. Every muscle was pronounced with the way she was dressed. All he could see was her blue eyes. As blue as any ocean that he'd ever flown over. When she came toward him, walking in the way only a woman who wore heels could do, she hit him in the face with the butt of her weapon.

"You like my suit? I've never worn anything like this before. But I got it from a good friend of mine to use. She said that since you'd been looking for me, you'd know me, but this way, I'd not leave any trace of me behind when I was finished with you. And there'd be no messy blood for me to clean off me." She moved around, stretching her legs and arms, making the fabric take on different proportions around her body. "Oh, I'm supposed to tell you that I borrowed this from Cora Banks."

Every cell in his body stopped moving. Just hearing the name of the worst hit man employed by the United States scared even his biological makeup. This woman laughed, as if she knew the other woman had scared him. It had too.

"I have money." She told him she didn't need the money. "Sure you do. Everyone needs money." Conley looked at Patty. "Kill her, and I'll make it worth your while. I'll give you half of everything I own."

"I'm the king of faeries. My mate is back with me. I already have it all. There is nothing else I need in the world but that." Patty laughed. "You, however, no longer have money. Nor do you have anything in the way of possessions. Your home is being searched as we speak by some very thorough people. We've taken care that all your little schemes are ready to put out into the world, and all will see what sort of little shit you are. So no, nothing you have is anything that I want."

"You can't do that to me. I'm too important of a man to have people like you around me. Much less— How did you find my things?" It was the woman in black that told him. "What were you doing snooping around in my things? It's not as if I laid out my passwords for you to find. You're going to be in huge trouble when I get out of this room."

"You're not." It made his dick hurt it was curled so tightly against his ass when the very man he'd been looking to kill came out of the darkened corner. "Hello, Parker. I've heard you're looking for me. What is it I can do for you?"

"Die." That slipped out before he could think it might be the wrong word to use. But almost as soon as he said it, he was glad for it. "You and the other undercover agents are in the way. I'm not going to have one of you sneaking up on me when I'm dictator and blowing my head off."

"You mean like today." Again, he thought his cock was trying to hide up his ass. "However, you'll be happy to know that neither Paige nor I are going to kill you. It will look like you've killed yourself, but you won't have the chance to do that. Mildred is going to kill you in her own way, so you suffer as much as she did at your hands. And we're all thrilled to death that we don't have to go through all the hard work to make it so you're dead and out of the way. This way, magic will make you dead, and nothing will come back to bite us in the ass."

"Why are you doing this to me?" No one said a word. "Where is Paige? You mentioned her. Is she your wife? Perhaps she can be talked to. Let me talk to her."

"Paige is my sister. And you have spoken to her, moron." He nodded to the woman in black. Christ, could this be any worse? he thought. He told James he didn't know who she was. "She's not on anyone's books. Paige has been getting in and out of situations since before you decided to be stupid. Although, I think you've been stupid since you took your first breath. You'll also be happy to know that she was there with her mate when you decided to go to the pub we were in and kill everyone. Also, we've found the body of the operative you had set up to take me down."

"How is that possible? There isn't any way she was able to slip through my fingers like this. I demand you tell me what is going on, and to release me before I call in someone to have you all arrested." No one moved to do what he wanted. When the room around him seemed to tighten up, like something took all the air out of the room, he looked at the woman he'd held to keep Patty in line. "What is going on now? You can't be serious about any of this."

The moment he realized he was really going to die was when something tore at his body. Looking down at himself, he could see that his legs, both of them, were gone from the knees down. The only way they'd make this look like anything but murder was to use magic. And he was learning the hard way that this being had more than she needed to make his death look like anything she wanted it to. Blood was pooling under him at a rapid rate, and he knew he was as good as dead if he didn't do something soon.

"I think we got off on the wrong foot here." Another slash of her magic or whatever it was tore his belly open. His guts were pouring out of him onto his lap. Conley was getting dizzy now and wasn't sure he could speak. "I don't want to die. Please, don't kill me."

"Too late." Almost as soon as he realized what she was saying, he felt himself being torn apart. Not just his legs and his belly, but his arms and the top of his head were falling onto the floor around him. Weak with the pain and loss of blood, he couldn't even make a sound when he realized he was going to die. "Oh, you're right on that, Conley. However, you're already dead."

Weakness took him under. Just when he thought he was dead, something would touch him — magic, he'd come to discover — and he'd be brought back to the present. While still in pain, it was tolerable. Something he could face. Each time he just wanted to end this nightmare, the woman would bring him around long enough to hurt him again and again. Death, he thought, had never been something he'd thought of, but right now, he'd give just about anything to end his life.

Sliding into his death finally was something he never thought he'd be happy about. All his planning seemed secondary to wanting to die. Just as he was slipping away, he had a single thought. He should have never messed with Patty and his mate.

Chapter 7

Paige laid the babies on the blanket she'd brought out to the backyard. Mary and Angel were at the packhouse for a while, and she was alone in the big house. The day, while it was mid-October, had turned into a beautiful warm afternoon. The babies seemed to be enjoying the trees swaying and the leaves falling to the ground. However, she knew that in no time, they'd be sound asleep. Babies slept a great deal, she'd come to realize.

"May I have a seat with you?" Smiling up at her sister-in-law, she told Shannon she'd love that. "Your brother is trying my patience, and I want to brain him. How is your afternoon? Better than mine, I'm thinking."

"More than likely, I'd agree with you. However, I know for a fact that James is having some difficulty wrapping his head around how easy it was to be able to explain away the suicide of Parker." She said she'd not thought it would have been something anyone would have cared about. "That was it. I think he's wondering if his own death will be just as overlooked. I told him I'd be dancing a jig. Of course, that didn't set well with him either. Have you found a house? Or is that what has him giving you fits?"

"The house. The two he's narrowed it down to are larger than life if you were to ask me. One has nine bedrooms, the other eleven. However, in the eleven bedroom one, he wants to have the three bedrooms for his kids enlarged to take up three of the extra. They are sort of small in that you couldn't park a car in them." She laughed with Shannon. "I would love the extra room. I'll admit that. I don't have any family left, nor do you two, I guess. But the extended family with the Marshalls is something I'd not counted on. They're just basically large all the way around, aren't they?"

"They are. I guess Shep, being the oldest son, is larger than most of his brothers. However, Rebel's husband is bigger still because he's her familiar. There is a great deal of magic going on around here too." She nodded, and Paige looked down at her sleeping children. "Will you guys want to have more children? I know that Heath and I want some, but it might be a few years. Having four children at one time without any kind of setup is a lot for anyone to handle. However, Heath makes it easy for me. I guess for both of us. He's a great hands on kind of dad. The older two are starting to trust him, which is saying a great deal. The babies won't know him as anything other than their dad. I honestly never thought I'd have children. I didn't think I'd live that long. Because of my job."

"James told me you were good at what you do." She shrugged. "He also told me that you'd try to hide your professionalism under a light."

"Not that. I just don't know many people who are actually aware of what I do. I mean, very few people in the White House have any idea who I am and that I'm able to get in and out of situations better than most. I've just thought of it as a job that I can do well. And I do." She glanced at Shannon. "Have you heard much about Sara, James's first wife?"

"Just a little. He told me they were more used to being together than they were in love. I found that hard to believe. He's so passionate about things." When her face pinked up, Paige chose to ignore it for now. "I guess you and she were friendly."

"I don't know that I'd call it friendly. We, like James and her, tolerated each other. When the kids came along, it was easier. They were a buffer. I never thought Sara was good enough for my brother."

Paige amended that when she realized what she'd said. "Being good enough isn't the right word for that. She was a snob. Even before the money that James had invested for them started to make a dent in their mortgage and other bills. Then when they no longer needed to have two jobs to make the rent, she took being a stay at home mom to a whole new level. Like she acted like she invented being a mom and wrangling two kids. Billy was only a baby when she was killed."

"I'm sorry to hear that. When I was talking to Beth with the ship to shore phone call last night, she didn't even want to talk to me about me moving into Sara's position." Paige said it had little to do with her being her stepmom. "Then what? I don't want to start off on the wrong footing with his children. It's hard enough being a mate to someone, I'm thinking, without mixing up the waters with trouble between the kids."

She thought about what she could tell the other woman. Things that she wasn't sure James even knew. But Beth had shared some things with her that she was sure that James would be royally pissed about, even though Sara was dead, enough to have him digging her up and arguing with her about it even after all this time.

"Beth was nine years old when she came to me in

the middle of the night one night. Her dad and I hadn't been home all that long together, a couple of days, I guess. I had a month off for resting up, and James was at the end of his R&R. Only about two days left. I'd been shot and was recuperating. He was just taking some personal time off. I found out later it was to deal with something to do with Sara." Paige looked out over the grass and into the deep woods, not sure how much she wanted to tell Shannon. Then Paige figured what the hell, she needed to be on a good relationship with Beth so that the girl would have a friend when she needed one. "Jamie was seven at the time, so he wasn't as aware of things going on around the house as much as Beth was. Her mother, wanting to have a friendship with Beth instead of a mother/daughter kind of one, would tell her daughter everything. Too much, as it turned out. Sara had had an abortion while James was away. Sara had gone into great detail with Beth on whose baby it was and what having an abortion felt like. There were more stories like that Beth shared with me while sobbing about how she didn't want to know her mom's life. Not to say that Beth didn't want a good relationship with her mom, but not to the point that it had come. So I told Beth to simply walk away. Or to tell her no, she didn't want those kinds of stories. For Christ's sake, the kid was only nine years old. Much too young to know details like she was getting. Beth did what I suggested, and their relationship on all levels seemed to dry up."

Shannon didn't say anything but did pick up Emma when she started to fuss. A leaf had blown into her face and startled her awake. Paige waited for her to speak before she told her the last part of the story.

"James didn't like his wife at all." That wasn't a surprise to Paige, but what she'd told her next was. "Jamie isn't James's. He knows that. They both do, as a matter of fact. Like you, he'd never treat his son any differently than you would the four that you have when you give birth to more children. However, Sara told him the night before she was killed that she was going to take the kids from him, including Billy, and run off where he'd never find them. I don't know what one had to do with the other in leaving him, but she was packed and ready to go when she was killed. The day you saw her at the airport when she was killed was her heading out to find a place for her and the kids to live. I wonder now if she ever had any plans to return for them."

"I did wonder about that for years. Why she was there. I knew she couldn't have been there to meet me, as no one knew where or when I'd be coming in from. Not to mention she waved at me, or in my general direction, I guess, like she'd not seen me in years." Paige laughed a little. "She was more than likely meeting someone there, and I just happened to be in the airport. For all I know, she didn't even see me at all. I did kill her killers, but there was never an inquiry about who or what had been going on. Not a word was mentioned about it afterwards either."

"I don't know. But you've made me think I can make this work with James. He was upset with me when I left, but I think it had more to do with the money he was willing to spend on a house when we'd just met. Do cats mate for life?" Paige told her she didn't know about wild animals, but shifters of all kinds did. "He told me that too, but I wasn't sure what to believe. It's a great deal to get tossed at you at one time."

"Believe me when I tell you, I understand that perfectly." The babies were wide awake, as awake as two and a half week olds could be, and they gathered them up to take inside. Emma needed her diaper changed, and George was just fussy. Paige nearly dropped George when Mildred stood up from the table in the dining room. "I didn't know you were coming. I'm sorry."

"I didn't know myself until I saw you two coming into the house. We have a gift for you and the others. I'd like to— Knowing them the way we've come to know them, they'll not think they need to be thanked for their parts in the way they helped Patty and I. But you've saved my life. And his. We need to thank you in some way." Paige told the faerie queen she felt the same way. They didn't need thanks. "But you must take it. I can understand not needing anything more in the way of tangible gifts or money, but what we will be giving you will be something you will use for years to come. Please. Could you please talk to your family and tell them we'd like to meet with them?"

"I can do that. And we'll gather together. But as for taking the gift, that will be wholly up to them." Paige handed today's paper to the older woman. "Did you see this? It came off just as Rebel said it would. That Conley Parker committed suicide. It also says he did it in his beloved offices, as that was the only place he felt at home. The mother fucker."

Mildred laughed, and Paige and Shannon joined her. "Who is it that you'd like to have there, my lady? You do know that the patriarch is not here and won't be for a few more weeks." She said that she and Patty would get with the other three later. "All right. If you'll just let me know when you'd like for us to all get together, then we can do that for you."

"Tonight. Unless you'd like for Patty to just give it to you without any kind of explanations. He'd do that too. I've never seen him so excited about something before." Mildred stood and smiled at them. "I must get going. As I said, if you can manage to make it for this evening, that would be good. The two of us can show up at any time you wish."

"Tonight it is. I'm sure they're all wanting to get together anyway. It's been a couple of days since we've all had a meal together. They enjoy that a great deal." They did too. Paige had never seen a family as close as this one was. "I'll have them here at six. I'd like it if you could join us for dinner too."

"Gladly. All right. I'll see you then. By the way, Shannon, you are as much a part of the Marshall shadow as the rest of them are, so I do hope you and James will be there as well. Bring little Billy. He is a delight to speak to and to have around us." Shannon said she'd make sure they were there. "Good. I have a special gift for him too. Nothing like what Patty and I are giving the adults, but this will be something that will help him when he's out and about."

Thanking her, Paige looked at Shannon when Mildred left. "Do you know what she's talking about? I mean, she made it sound like Billy needs something to keep him safe. Has something happened?" Shannon said she had no idea. "Me either. But I guess we'll find out. All right. I have to contact the others. You tell James that you're eating here. Now I have to figure out— You know what? We're going to order all kinds of food and have it delivered. Anything and everything that we can order. Pizza to gourmet sounds wonderful. And easy cleanup."

"You need a cook." Paige knew that but didn't want to give up her time with just the six of them in the house in the evening. "Think about how much more time you'll have than you have now when you just walk away from the table when you're finished. You don't have to worry about cooking it up either. The one that James has been using is wonderful. I love having my tea and eggs cooked just perfectly for me when I get up in the morning."

"I'll talk to Heath about it. He seems to enjoy cooking for us when I've been out all day." Shannon pointed out that with Heath being home when she got home, he could hold her rather than having to worry about food and such. "You're right. I guess I didn't want to give anything up to have him around. I will talk to him when we have the house to ourselves after tonight. I have been looking for nannies too. Harris is helping me with that. She's looking for one as well."

It took the two of them nearly an hour to order food. There was going to be a lot of varieties for dinner, mostly because she'd ordered while hungry. So instead of ordering with her head, she let her hungry belly do the deciding. Everything was to arrive at six, so she had just over two hours to kill before everyone started to arrive. With the babies down for their endless nap time, she got on her computer and began looking things up that the house still needed. An email hit her inbox just as she opened up the program to verify her orders. It was from the president.

"I hope it's all right that I email you with this address. I'm never sure what I'm supposed to do when I'd like to thank someone for the clandestine work they've done for myself and their country. I know you had a hand in taking care of the recent trouble — I had no idea that anyone was up to so much again — and I thank you for all of that." She wondered if he realized he hadn't mentioned names. More than likely, he did. He was covering his tracks as well. "There are several things I'd like to speak to you about. Not just you, but the rest of the family. Nothing bad, just a simple thank you in person for your help. Let me know if there is a way for me to do this without blowing anything up for you and your lovely family."

Just as Paige was trying to figure out if this was something that she needed to be concerned about, someone rang the doorbell. She was surprised to find Billy standing there, and he looked like he'd taken quite a beating.

"What the hell happened to you?" He stomped into the house and headed to the kitchen. She followed, glad now that Shannon had left. "I asked you a—"

"I need a cookie or something." She pulled the

cookie jar that Heath had only just filled this morning down and handed him one. "I was knocked around for trying to save a girl. She didn't want to be saved, I guess, and she punched me in the nose. Girls are weird. Not you, Aunt Paige, but girls are weird."

"I see." She handed him two more cookies. "What was happening that you thought she needed saving from?"

"Two boys. I thought they were hurting her. She sure was making enough noise about them touching her, but I guess that was her deal." He told her again that girls were weird. "Anyway, I knocked the one boy back on his butt by punching him in the face, and the other one ran off screaming about how he didn't want his face messed up too. You know what, Aunt Paige, all humans are weird."

"I think you might be right. So this girl, instead of thanking you for helping her out, she hit you. Billy, you're just too nice of a guy. I love that about you, but you're a romantic in an unromantic world." She got up to get a washcloth so he could wipe the blood off his face. "You're healing already, so just clean up. We're having dinner here tonight, so why don't you call Shannon or your dad and let them know you're here?"

After he got off the phone, getting approval for the stayover, he helped her put out dishes and silverware. The two of them talked about all sorts of things, including Shannon. He seemed genuinely happy that Shannon was going to be a part of his and his family's life now. The kid had a heart of gold. She just hoped no woman, human or not, crushed it someday.

~*~

Heath was stuffed. There had been just enough food for him to get a bit of everything and still be full at the end. He loved meals like this one. Not all the time, mind, but once in a while, he enjoyed having a lot of things to put on his plate that had nothing to do with each other. When the dishes were loaded into the dishwasher, he and Paige started putting things away.

"We should hire a cook." He said that was a wonderful idea. "Don't just agree with me. Tell me what you think."

"I really think we need a cook. I love cooking for you guys, but I'd also like to not have to, especially when the kids are getting ready to go out for the day. It's as hectic as I thought it would be. Or more so, really." She nodded, and he asked her what else was wrong. "There is something, correct?"

"Yes. This gift thing with Patty and his wife. They did most of the work, and now they want to gift us something that I feel we don't need." Heath agreed with her but also told her what he'd heard about not accepting the gift they had. "It's considered rude to not accept a gift from someone, and it's not all right to not accept one. That's just fucked up — you know that, don't you?"

"Yes." They were both laughing when Shep came into the kitchen to tell them it was time. Leaving the work for later — there wasn't really that much — Heath was glad they were going to start hiring staff. He wanted to have some fun with the family now that he had one, and having to keep up with the house was taking time away.

Sitting in the living room, he noticed a couple of things that had changed since he left the living room. There was a fireplace in the room, as well as more floor to ceiling windows. It was nice but unexpected. He wondered if that was the gift. Heath thought he could live with that.

"I have a gift for each of you as couples. Also, for young Trenton. He will, when his mate arrives, share with her. But for now, I would like to give you them." Patty was very giddy at what he was going to do, and Heath felt it touch him as well. "I will start with the first male to be born to the family and go from there. Shep — "

"I'm sorry. I'm not being rude here, but why the males? You said it was for us as a couple. I'm sorry.

That didn't come out right. It sounded worse than it sounded in my head." Mildred explained. "Oh. I guess I never thought of that. Male to male talking and giving of the gifts or whatever won't have me wanting to tear your throat out. Even if I could. Yes, we cats are a jealous lot. I agree with your reasoning about giving the males the gift. Thank you so much. Doing it this way will make me feel a good deal less like I need to hurt you."

"Thank you." Patty shivered, he was so excited, and Heath had to laugh at his brother when he looked around like he was expecting the Spanish Inquisition to come into the house with them. "For you, Shep, I give you Banana. He is a loyal and wonderful—"

"You can't give us a person." Heath looked at Harris when she burst out with that. "I mean, it's nice of you and all, but you can't just give us a person."

"It's not a person." Patty was getting frustrated, and everyone could see it. "If you'd allow me to finish this, I'm sure you'll understand completely. I give you Banana. He is a loyal and wonderful faerie that has an army of his own that he can call upon to keep you safe. I give him to you to use as you wish. To call upon him for help that you'd not otherwise be able to get. He will have magic, a great deal of it, to be able to call upon the army he has at a moment's notice, and to be able to do whatever is needed for you to keep all you have safe. Including the babes you'll have."

He spoke to his brothers in turn. Each of them were given a faerie, each with an army to call upon. When he got to Dean and Rebel, he bowed before them. He told them how they'd given him his life back, given him his all by saving his mate.

"I give to you the richest gift that a king can bestow upon another. I give to you both the job of king and queen of the faeries. Not to say that I have any intentions of retiring soon. But it will make my heart rest easier knowing that someone as strong and as good hearted as the two of you are will be able to easily step into our shoes to make things right." Rebel pointed out that she was already in charge of witches. "Yes, and that job will give you so much when you take over our kingdom for us. But as I said, not for a great many years from now."

There was little for them to say. Little, Heath thought, that they knew to say. An army apiece to call upon? A faerie that would belong to both people in a relationship? What sort of thing would have to happen for them to have the need to call upon six armies? There were too many questions without answers, but he was sure it, like all the other magic they were given, would be something that would sort itself out eventually.

When Mildred sat before Billy, Heath felt

himself tense up. The little boy had made his way deep into his heart, and he didn't want anything to happen to him. Even if it was just overwhelming him.

"Several days ago, you came to see me while I rested by the waterway at the end of the property here. You and I had a very long talk, mostly to do with how your family was all out vacationing, and you were stuck at home." Billy's face turned bright red as he turned and looked at his dad. "I'm sure they understand, as I said to you before, that you're a bit lonely with your brother and sister being gone. I have a gift and a bit of magic that I'd like to bestow upon you for cheering me up. And making me laugh when I thought I'd never feel like laughing again."

"You did look sort of sad." Everyone laughed until Billy glared at them. "She was sitting by the water just staring at it like she wanted to just jump in and drown herself. Of course, I talked to her."

"And you did a good thing for my mate, Billy. A very good thing. Every day that she is feeling low, less and less thanks to your visits to her, she tells me something you said to her. Or an observation you have. You are a brilliant young man." Billy thanked Patty. "You're so very welcome. Now, let's give you what you need."

Mildred took his hand into hers. "This is a faerie. She was born at the exact time that you were,

on the same date and year. She is forever your faerie."
The tiny little faerie lay still in the queen's hand until
Billy put out his own hand. It flew right to him and
sat down. "She has no name as yet. Sometimes they
choose their own names when they are older, but I have
given her permission to be named by you. It's a very
important thing to name a faerie. It's why they wait
until they're older, at least a hundred years old, until
they choose one for themselves. That way, they have
a knowledge of the world around them and a better
understanding of what they're good at. This little one
has been told that she will be your companion, as well
as a guide to the world around you."

"Like that cricket in the whale movie." Mildred
said that was it precisely. "I'm going to name her
Cricket. That way, when I think about her, I'll know
she's going to help me make smart decisions."

Cricket pulled out a tiny blade from the
air. When Mildred explained that they'd need to
exchange blood to be able to talk, Billy did so without
any hesitation. When he asked if he could go outside,
Patty told him that he had a gift for him as well.

"It is the ability to speak to all creatures. Not
just your own faerie, but anything that has a spirit.
Trees, plants, living things that you might not think
are alive. All things that you wish to speak to, or need
information from, will be able to converse with you

without any troubles." Billy asked why he thought he'd need that. "Because, young Billy, you will be able to go beyond helping your family in things that matter. You'll be able to find things that are lost for decades and beyond. Find bodies that will aid others in taking care of crimes. You will, my friend, be the greatest addition to the earth that anyone will ever see again."

"Wow." Everyone laughed, and it embarrassed Billy. "I don't know what to say, Mr. Patty. That's a powerful thing to have. Shouldn't somebody older have something like that?"

"I've picked the perfect person for it, I know." Billy thanked Mildred as well, and then he and Cricket took off for the outside. "I can only imagine what the two of them will be doing for the next few days. Pestering every living creature, testing out their magic."

They talked until very late. The babies were fed by the family, and they seemed to be having a good time with them. Mary and Angel enjoyed playing with Billy, who was, shockingly, willing to share what he'd been able to figure out with the magic. Angel seemed to have a slight crush on the young man, but she was only a child, and he was like a big brother, he supposed.

After they all left them and the children were

in bed, he found himself back in the living room after clean up, just holding Paige. It had been a very long day, and he was just too tired to move at the moment.

"I heard from the president today. He wants to come here or meet somewhere, I guess, to thank us personally for what we did. I'm not sure I believe it was him, so I'm going to slip in and out of his offices to see. I don't like that he emailed me for some reason." He asked her if she was just being paranoid. "More than likely. But it's better to be safe than in an ambush that I could have prevented. It won't be that bad, I don't think. Easy in and out."

"Just be careful." She said she would. It was then that Carrot—such an odd name for a faerie, he thought—told them that he could go and see what was up. "That's wonderful if Paige is onboard with that."

Carrot left them then and said he'd return in the morning unless there was trouble. He and Paige were headed up to bed at two in the morning, and Heath was about as happy as he'd ever been. As soon as he laid his head on the pillow, not another thought entered his tired mind.

Chapter 8

Paige didn't know where she was for several seconds. She knew she'd gone to bed with Heath, but now she was doing that out-of-body thing again. When Heath came out of the next room, she was glad to see him. Then something occurred to her.

"Where are—? Who is with the children?" Carrot came buzzing at her, and she put the question to him. "The other time we left the house, or whatever we're about, there wasn't anyone we had to worry about. Now we have four children at home, and we're here." She looked around. "Where is here anyway?"

"The White House, my lady. And the children are being taken care of as if you're there with them. The faeries, you see. They'll watch them in the same way you would if the two of you were there with them." Not that she didn't believe him, but she pointed out they were a great deal smaller than the babies. "They are. But they're magical. Changing diapers, feeding them, they'll just use their magic to make those things better for them. They are, as I said, as safe as they'd be if you were there with them."

"Are we not at home?" She looked at Heath—his voice sounded a little stressed. "Will someone go into our home if they can't contact us and find us in bed? Will they believe we're dead? I don't know that I've given this as much thought as I should have. I'm not sure if I could have kept myself at home, but I don't want my family to be freaked out."

"The faeries will take care that no one disturbs you, Lord Heath. But you being here is very important to you both. I would like for you to meet Cobalt. His duty is to care for Larry Householder, the new president of the United States. He's doing a good job so far, I believe. He is the man you were talking about earlier, correct?" Paige said that was it. "Cobalt has been with him since his master was a child."

"Longer than that, you old turd. Why are you here in the middle of the freaking night?" Carrot told him to behave. "I'll not. You're in my home and bothering me. Not the— Who is this you have here? They're night watchers, them are. My goodness. I've not seen the likes of you since…well, it's been a long time. Whatcha here for?"

Paige started to answer Cobalt when she was

cut off as Carrot started yelling at the other faerie.

"I'm trying to tell you what they're here for and explain to them why they can do this. At least I was until you came in here flapping your mouth—"

Cobalt cut Carrot off this time. "I'd not have to be flapping my mouth at anything if you'd given me warning they were coming here. Holy Jehoshaphat, you've not changed one bit, have you? In all my life, I've never—"

Paige whistled. Both the little faeries turned and looked at her.

"We're here now, so how about you tell us what has brought us here? And be nice about it." Both of them pointed to the other. "I don't care what is going on between the two of you, but I will put my foot down on one of you if you don't act right. It's been pointed out that it's the middle of the night. Yes. I would like to go back to my bed too. So why the hell are we here?"

"She's got herself a fine temper on her, don't she?" Cobalt poked Carrot as he continued talking about her. "I don't know that I'd want her to put her foot on me, but she sure is a looker, Carrot. My goodness."

"Now, don't be eyeing my mistress like that. She's the mate to a fine family of jaguars. You behave."

Cobalt, of course, took exception to being told

to behave and started up again. Paige just walked away and into what she thought was the living room of the personal quarters of the president.

Heath was laughing when he caught up with her. "They'll be at it all night if we were to let them. I remember having those sorts of arguments with my brothers when I was younger. Mom would hose us down with her watering hose. No matter the weather, she'd squirt that thing right at us. You can bet we straightened up after that. What did he mean that we're night watchers?"

"I don't know. I mean, I've never been able to just assume a role in something else that was going on before I met you. I understand the term, but I'm wondering if we can only do this at night. It's something we'll have to figure out." Carrot sat on her shoulder. "Are you two finished?"

"He's gone away. He didn't believe I was working directly with the king and queen on this with you. I guess he went to find out." Heath asked to have Cobalt come here to talk to him. "I don't wish to cause any trouble, sir. He'll figure it out or not."

"Now is as good a time as any. Besides, if we must come back here again, I don't want anyone thinking you're not doing a good job. Call for him, and we'll get this finished, so we don't have to worry about him making trouble for any of us." When Carrot left, Paige asked Heath what he was going to do. "Fix this so that we don't have any trouble with anyone we visit. I'd like to go someplace and not have to worry about stepping on anyone's toes."

Cobalt came back with Carrot, and they were arguing again. This time it seemed to be more serious. Cobalt was actually accusing Carrot of having no rights to be in his home and that he was going to have him banished as soon as he could. Heath simply lifted his hand, then snapped his fingers. Suddenly Patty was there with his lovely wife.

"Couldn't get enough of me, could you? Well, what is it—? What's amiss around here? I feel hatred and meanness. What is this about?" When Cobalt started to explain his version of what was happening, so did Carrot. Although Carrot's version was truer to what was happening, the other faerie was louder and kept bumping Carrot with his large belly. "Enough."

Patty's voice was thunderous. The faeries fell to the floor and bowed before their king. Mildred told them both to rise but to keep their mouth shut. She didn't sound all that happy with the two little men.

"What is the meaning of this, Cobalt?" As the faerie began explaining, again, his version of the reason Patty had been summoned, Carrot didn't speak. "So, you took it upon yourself to keep these two people from their jobs simply because you were not warned about them being around. Do you think I'm to give you a heads up, you called it when I have an idea to make our lives better? Do you suppose I should run my ideas past you so they can have your stamp of approval before moving forward? Think carefully on that question, Cobalt."

"I don't know that you should do that, no." Patty growled. "No. No, you need not have to run things by me. But they didn't tell me they were coming."

"Nay, they'd not. As night watchers, they go where the night needs them. And it was here that they were to come. How do you suppose that would work if they were to come to a place where they are needed and ran into someone like you, questioning their every move? Did you not recognize them as such? As the night watchers? I'd like to think they are well marked in that area. Or is it that you didn't see a mark on young Carrot here, and assumed, badly so, that he wasn't with them?" Patty licked his thumb and pressed it against the chest of Carrot. The little guy was shocked back from whatever happened. "There. Are you satisfied? He is now marked as the keeper of the night watchers. There will be no more talk about how he isn't to be here. Do you understand me? Or do I have to make an example of you in this?"

"No, sir. Don't do that." They all turned to Carrot. "He was only protecting what he has come to love. I should have thought of that as well. I wish no harm to come to Cobalt for protecting his realm here and the man that he is assigned to."

"You have a good heart, Carrot. There should be more understanding faeries like you around." Mildred turned to them. "You go about your business here, Paige and Heath. The rest will work itself out. We'll need to mark all the helpers of the others as well, I think. I'd not want anyone unable to do their jobs if this were to come up again."

The two of them went deeper into the living room. There wasn't much to see—the rooms were just as ordinary as their own was at home. It wasn't until they entered a smallish office that they saw the president bent over a computer.

Going up behind him, unsure if they could be seen or not, Paige read the things he had on his screen. While Heath did the same thing, she looked at his desk, the notes he'd been making, as well as the clippings he had cut from some print-offs he'd done. Just as she was going to ask Heath what he thought they were doing here, Larry turned toward them.

They stared at each other for several seconds before Larry put out his hand like he was trying to make sure they were actually there. When his hand went through her, Paige knew the man was stressed to the point of being ill about it. She also understood

176 Kathi S. Barton

why they were there.

"I don't understand." Heath introduced the two of them to the other man and told him they were night watchers. "You're here to kill me? I've done nothing wrong. However, it would end a great deal of stress for me if I were to be hurt enough to chill out."

His smile was short lived when Paige spoke. "We're only here to see what we can do to help you. And I believe we can." Larry turned back to the computer, telling them the things he'd found when he'd been taking a tour around the White House. "There are ways for us to get in and out of places without anyone knowing it. Let me take a quick look at the room you've discovered today. And the things that are in it. It might only be a storage place and has been forgotten."

"I'd like that very much if it were true."

She disappeared in that moment, ending up outside of a room on the lower levels of the large building. Walking through the walls was something she'd not been able to do before, and it was sort of weird. But she was able to see things she doubted anyone else could see. Even armed with a flashlight and a book, Paige thought the room would look just as Larry had thought it would.

The furniture was covered, and there was a thick film of dust over it. Paintings laid against the wall, some of them looking as if they had only just been put in here compared to the others around them. In the corners were boxes of books, labeled from where they'd come from. Even dishes as well as other breakable items were sitting on dusty shelves as if the person who had brought them had forgotten to wrap them up and put them in a box. Paige made her way back to the office.

"You thought the house was being robbed, I'm assuming." He told her how he'd seen where things were added to the room. Larry had been afraid that Conley had been stockpiling things to remove. And he was wondering what other things he might have actually taken out. "It's all storage from rooms you now occupy. Like paintings you have replaced with something you brought. Dishware sets too. If there wasn't an object you brought in to fill a space, the paintings that were there would have been set up. Dishes as well. Your wife, she must have packed everything up to move in here, and they put the other things away so as not to crowd you."

"The books too. I did wonder why the previous president hadn't set up his own library, and my books were put there." Larry laughed, but it sounded like an embarrassed laugh. "This all happened so quickly that I'm still working my way through things here. Anna too. She's been asking about certain things she thought she'd brought, and they've been put into storage until she told them where she wanted her things put. I should have thought of that instead of jumping to the wrong conclusion."

"No, never stop thinking hard on things. You are coming into this place where the country was in peril. You needed us, and this was just a start, I think, of us being able to help you." Larry said it was sort of a silly thing for them to come here for. "Perhaps, but you'll sleep better knowing the answer. Also, I'm thinking this was a way for us to meet without anyone knowing about it. We need to figure out a way we'll be able to communicate without using computers. I want you to be safe."

All they needed to do was touch, which was odd too when she thought about it. They couldn't actually touch—she and Heath weren't physically there. But they could do a magical touch with their hands. With their fingers at each other's wrists, they would slide them over their fingertips. That was all it took, and now they had a connection that would help them in the future.

They talked about different things he was doing right now, two more things she and Heath were able to help him with, and a couple he was nearly finished looking into. It was nice that they felt so good around him. There wasn't a sense of distrust from the man, and she had a feeling their magic was making it possible for them to see his true self. Anna joined them as the sun was coming up. Paige liked her as well.

"We're just a couple of people that want to make this world a better place to live in. Never in a million years did we expect to be living in this big house." Paige told Anna that she believed they'd make it work. "I hope so. I never knew there was so much red tape to get things going. My goodness. There are times when I just want to skip asking about something and get it going. But I also know that would make quite a few people unhappy with me."

"I'm sure that if you let us know, we can help you out with a lot of the projects you have going. My family has been doing things like you're talking about for some time now. We could, perhaps, get something started for you, and you can implement it into one of your projects. That way, it's tried, and you know it will work." Heath looked at her before continuing. "Paige and I have a connection with Larry now, so we should have one with you as well. Then I believe we need to get home to our babies. They might be missing us about now."

After the touch to her hand, she and Heath woke up in their bed. The funny thing was, they were both rested, not feeling at all as if they'd spent most of the night out and about. Smiling to herself, Paige went to check on the children and found that Carrot had been right. They were about as safe as anyone could have made them. There must have been two thousand faeries in the room with them, and all of them keeping a close eye on all four of them.

~*~

Trenton wasn't sure what he was going to do with such a large house, but he decided bigger was better in this family. Laughing to himself, he walked around the kitchen once more to try and figure out what he could dick around on the price. As he was thinking of making an offer, Harris contacted him.

Don't make an offer on it. I'd not even want the place after the things I've found out about it. He asked her what she'd found. *Two things I've been able to find out about the house is that it has about ten grand of unpaid taxes on it. They're going to try and make you be responsible for them. Also, the house, as you know, has been on the market for a while. I just found out the reason for it. Apparently, at one time, there were about seventy bodies buried all over the land, and they believe some are still there. At some point — and I'd more than likely think the real estate office knows this — the government will go in and seize the house and lands to look around again. Perhaps even going so far as tearing the house down to look under the foundation.*

Aren't they suppose to tell you that? She said they might hint at it, but she doubted they'd be that forthcoming. *I see. So I'm walking away from it. I might take you up on the offer to having my house finished that I've been working on. At least it would be something I know all about.*

It's been worked on now. I knew as soon as I figured out the hidden things of the one you're in now that you'd say that. And I agree. It's better to know what you're getting into rather than lose it, all over some problems that come around all of a sudden. He thanked her. *When you meet your mate, Trenton, things are going to go much smoother. I know that things have been for me and the rest of the family. Even your brothers are much calmer than they were before, I've been told.*

I'm hoping that's the way things work out for me. I could use a little calmness in my life for a change. Not that I think I'll have it when I meet her, but you never know. Besides, everyone has children or is going to have them, and I'm not going to take the chance of not having someplace for them all to live when they get here. I'm not saying it will happen, but I'm more of a be prepared sort of person. She laughed with him. *To be honest, I'm excited about having a mate. Someone to be able to share a life with.*

It is a wonderful feeling.

He told the realtor that he didn't want the house and left her standing there trying to convince him that this was the perfect house for him. Trenton got into his car and left her standing there begging him, really begging him, to purchase it at a lower price.

All right. I'll let you get back to being the only bachelor in the family.

Instead of going back to his home to see what was going on, Trenton made his way to the schoolhouse that was going up. It was a huge project they were all doing, and he was happy there would be a place for the kids to have a safe environment. After having a look around there, he made his way to the old schoolhouse to see how the renovations were going there.

The classrooms were being fitted with a bathroom and shower. There would be two women per room unless they had other children. Then the family would share the room. He also liked that they were putting in a kitchen in the rooms. While only a refrigerator and a microwave, it was going to be nice for a person to have a small snack or two when they wished it.

"Hello, Mr. Marshall. Have you come by to see what we're doing?" He told Mr. Kyle that he was just being nosy. "Not a bad thing. Come on, let me show you what we've done with the kitchen and dining areas. I think your grandda had a good idea when he suggested the few things we've done. Makes it seem less sterile if you ask me."

He was happy too. Instead of having long

tables, as had been in the room for eating, there were small tables scattered all around the room. He could see them with tablecloths on them. A nice little candle. It was almost romantic, Trenton thought. There were larger tables, Kyle told him. Mostly, he'd bet, for a family. Even as he was being shown the kitchen area, Trenton knew his grandda had had a hand in designing this space as well.

"He said there should be a couple of open fridges for the people coming in late. The kitchen will be open for the three meals, of course. This way, anyone can come in and get them something to eat without having to go out." There were large places for drinks and such as well, he was told. "That there wall will have windows that show a garden. Anyone that wants to work in them—I'm told it's a nice stress reliever—can do that too. That grandda of yours, he sure is a smart fella. I hope you guys know that."

"I did know that, but I think we still underestimate him a little. I love all these ideas." There were others too. Things that would make the place look less and less like a refuge and give it more of a homey setting. "I think this will be a good safe place for women in trouble, don't you think?"

"Yes, sir. I do. I knew this girl once—that's all she was too, a child. She got herself in a family way, and her parents kicked her to the side of the road.

No help from them, nothing to do with her. About six months into her being in that delicate condition, someone killed her while she was living in a box under the bridge. A car did it—came right up on the curb and ran her over. Killed them both. You know what? Those parents of hers, they didn't even show up at the funeral. Said she'd made her bed." Trenton asked if they'd done it. "Not really, but they might as well have with them tossing her out. Poor thing. If she'd had a place like this, both of them would be all right today. Sad world we live in if you ask me."

He agreed with him. As they toured the rest of the place, he was shown what the plans were for the outbuildings. There were three of them—not huge, but big enough to use as a classroom, a skills building, and a place to do laundry and such. There was also going to be a very heavy duty fence around the entire compound that would keep most anyone out. Those that made it over the fence would meet up with the pack that would be roaming the lands both night and day.

Trenton made his way back to his place just as he realized he was getting hungry. Stopping by the deli, he got him a thick sub, as well as a cold drink. Sitting out in the unusually warm day, he was enjoying the day a great deal better than he thought he might have when he woke up this morning.

He'd had some terrible dreams. Few of his family knew he'd suffered with night terrors for his entire life. None of them, during the day, were anything he thought should have bothered him. But at night, he'd wake up with a scream coming out of his mouth and his entire body drenched in sweat. Trenton wondered what a mate would think about that.

Heath joined him at the table he was sitting at with his own sandwich and drink. "I thought I saw you. I was going to take this home to eat, but if you don't mind, I'll stick it out with you." Trenton told him he was already joining him. They both laughed. "I've two games finished up. The one I was working on for dementia patients is ready for testing, and the other, a children's game to help with counting money, is going on the market soon. If I don't have another buyer wanting first dibs. The sucker has only just been finished, and I have people fighting over it."

"Well, that's not a bad thing, is it?" They talked about everything, but not really anything at all. He did tell him of the ideas that Grandda had on the building they were working on and how much he loved them. "Also, my house is being finished up. Might as well be prepared, don't you think?"

"Yes. I'd say so." They were finished eating, and he asked him where Paige was. "She's working on something for Harris. I stay out of those conversations as much as I can. They're not at all nice to each other, and I don't want to get in the middle of anything. I think Shep does the same thing when they're together. I noticed he wasn't home either when I dropped Paige off."

"They are a little intense." Boy, was that an understatement. "I was thinking about the holidays last night. This will be our first without Mom. I don't know how to feel about it. I think I'm going to miss her ten times as much. She loved the holidays so much."

"She did. But I have a feeling she's going to be right there with us." Trenton nodded, too emotional to speak. "I love you, Trenton. Very much. I think I need to say that to all of you more often."

He agreed, and when they stood up to go their separate ways, they hugged tightly and for a long time. Trenton needed that. More than he'd come to realize, he needed to feel arms around him. He, too, was going to do it more often. Yes, he thought, he was going to hug more often, even if it was just a quick one.

AWARD WINNING, BESTSELLING AUTHOR

Kathi Barton, a winner of the Pinnacle Book Achievement award as well as a best-selling author on Amazon and All Romance books, lives in Nashport, Ohio, with her husband, Paul. When not creating new worlds and romance, Kathi and her husband enjoy camping and going to auctions. She can also be seen at county fairs with her husband, who is an artist and potter.

Her muse, a cross between Jimmy Stewart and Hugh Jackman, brings her stories to life for her readers in a way that has them coming back time and again for more. Her favorite genre is paranormal romance, with a great deal of spice. You can visit Kathi online and drop her an email if you'd like. She loves hearing from her fans. aaronskiss@ gmail.com.

Follow Kathi on her blog: http://kathisbartonauthor. blogspot.com/

www.ingramcontent.com/pod-product-compliance
Lightning Source LLC
Chambersburg PA
CBHW030225180626
46810CB00008B/2973